# ERIC
# THE
# RAIGON-TALTH

by
**A Isobel Sutcliffe**

*It is unwise to wound a witch, foolish
to kill a wizard and high treason to
murder your king; but theft of innocence
abandons the soul to evil.*

JaCol Publishing Inc.



ISBN: 978-1-946675-20-0
For information regarding permission, write to:

JaCol Publishing Inc.
195 Murica Aisle
Irvine, CA 92614
818-510-2898
Editor-in-Chief: Randall Andrews
Technical Editor: C.E. Hilburn
Illustrator: Eva Taylor
www.jacolpublishing.com

# ACKNOWLEDGEMENT

Dedicated to my family. To my brother, Dan, for his encouragement. To Randall Andrews, my editor and writing coach, thank you for your patience and inspiration. Eva Hilburn for the cover art and the format editing. To the beautiful people of Writers World, you inspire, educate, and amuse me.

# TOC

## Contents

# Map

Brimstone Archipelago
Isle of L'Ascarle
Bellcliff Is.
Crakk
Darnel Rock
OLDEGOTH
King's Port
Beacon Tower
PARINITH STRAIT
Rock of Alor
Mortliss
Strait of Glimuth
Dorcliff Is.
Dragon's Fall
Dorcliff Channel
THE SERASYAN SEA
Rock of Wycliff
SERASYA
Asvann
Brimstone Archipelago
Eald D'Árian
SEA OF ESKOVAAL
Yellowsill
Esca Haven
W
S
N
E

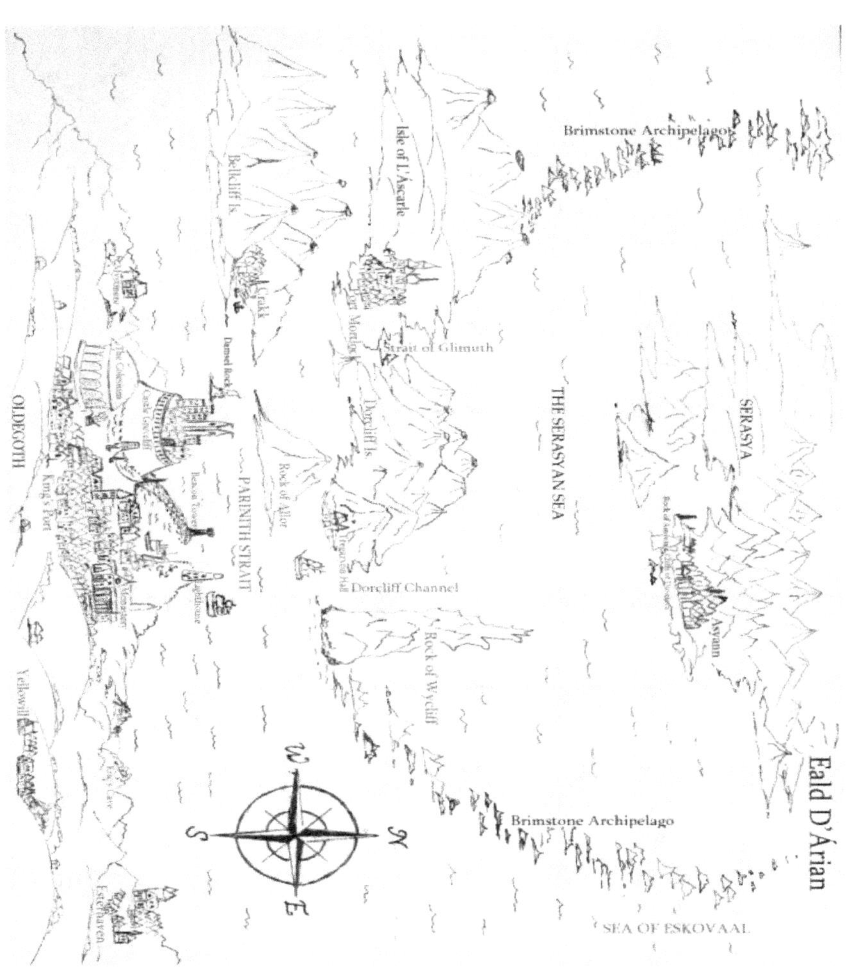

# 1

The Dead Bell rang and the Crier's voice echoed in the town square far below.

"Oyez! Oyez! Oyez!"

Crown Prince Raulin cradled his head; the next words would bring joy to many in the Kingdom—heartbreak to others.

"The King is dead! Long live the King!"

High above in the Keep another bell tolled twenty-six times—one for each year his father, King Eustace had ruled. The Herald's voice faded as he wound his way along Silversage Street to broadcast news of the King's death. The manner of his death would remain a secret to all but those closest and to those responsible.

Raulin turned to the window. The wind hammered Serasyan Sea—grey and cold—matched his mood. Petrels skimmed the whitecaps in their eternal quest for fish. Sails on the horizon heralded the arrival of a merchant ship bound for King's Port Harbour. A beacon tower stood at the seaward end of the breakwater, primed and ready to rally the people should danger loom.

*Heaven forbid I should command that beacon lit.*

Raulin's attention returned to his father stretched out on his bed; sparse white hair, sallow and blotched skin. Soon the undertaker would move King Eustace to the great hall where his subjects could file past and pay their respects.

*Or perhaps they'll check if he is really dead before they celebrate.*

Crossed on his chest, the iron fists that had ruled the Kingdom of Oldegoth lay still and pale. His watchful eyes closed forever. As the life left his body, King Eustace had passed Raulin the crown.

"Rule with pride and strength, my son."

Inside him, Raulin cried for his father and the magnitude of the task ahead. Sixteen—neither boy nor man. Raulin's head swivelled to the crown on the floor beside him. Made long ago in Serasya, from gold, silver, and precious gems, it glimmered in the dim chamber.

"I will wear it when need arises, father," Raulin whispered, "for only with reluctance will I assume the throne."

He scraped back his chair, stooped to hook a finger through the crown; he rose and strode from the room. Across the city, the cathedral bells rang a cacophonous melody of mourning.

Raulin hastened to his chambers, tossed the crown on a chair, grabbed a lantern. He wiped the blood from the door to his secret exit and unlocked it. His feet scuffed the stone stairs, down and down, then along the narrow tunnel. He ran, heedless of the mossy stones underfoot until he came to ascending stairs, up he climbed, two at a time and burst through the door.

"Larkin? Milo?" A voice from along the passage answered and he joined his friends. Raulin reeled at the pungent odour of the salve Milo used. "How is he?"

Draped in robes of dark green, Milo's tall frame bent over the bed, his white hair fluffed out around the black fez. The wizard turned to study Raulin; his blue eyes pierced him from between bifocals and craggy brow. Larkin sat beside the battered figure on the bed. His blond head bowed and elbows propped on his thighs.

Milo's soft voice filtered through his thick moustache. "He'll live but he has a fight ahead of him."

Raulin's shoulders slumped and he blew out a long sigh. "Thank heavens." He moved closer to the bed. "My father has passed."

"I'm sorry to hear that. Long live King Raulin." Milo straightened his tall frame. "Are you sound, Prince?"

Raulin nodded.

"The knights have warned us of impending threats. I fear your father's death is just the beginning. As you take the throne, you may face many long, arduous days."

"I'm as ready as I'll ever be." *King Raulin—why can't I just be Raulin?*

"I have spoken to Reeve Calder; Wizard Ferrick will be appointed your personal cook and valet. Calder will serve you as he did your father. We must exercise utmost caution with your safety."

Larkin lifted his head and leaned back. He gave Raulin a haunted smile. "Your first duty will be to submit to my father's demand, no?"

"I will afford your father the same cooperation as my father before me."

"Thank you. I fear my refusal to return will bring war to the world of Eald D'Árian, but if I do return our predicament might be much worse."

"There was more to my father's refusal than sheer obstinance?"

"I hold knowledge my father wants—needs—to achieve his lifelong dream to rule all of Eald D'Árian."

"How can you give him that knowledge?"

"I know where the so-called Golden Hall of Serasya is."

"What does he expect to find in there?"

"Inigo Thornfingers and his dragon."

"Ah! Of course! And Thornfinger's will give him powers beyond his wildest dreams."

Larkin chuckled. "My father seeks to use Thornfingers to help him achieve greatness. From what I have learned, if Thornfingers could return, he would use my father to accomplish his own goals and then kill him. My little brother is a believer too—silly fool. Every night, he lights a candle and prays to Lord Thornfingers, pleads with him to rise from The Golden Hall and make him able-bodied."

Raulin's mouth twitched. "Does he believe in Tagrali too?"

"Oh yes, keeps his window firmly locked, day and night."

"My au pair used to threaten me with Tagrali." Raulin pitched his voice to falsetto. "Be good or old Tagrali will come and take you away!"

Milo turned to his young companions and raised his shaggy eyebrows. "Behind every myth, there is an element of truth, boys."

# 2

Eric dreamed his mother sang to him, his father told him a tale of dragons and the fearsome Tagrali; the dream darkened, flames and cries of despair drowned his mother's song. A child cried, *'No, no—please—no! I don't want to go!'*

"Eric!" His sister, Cateline, shook him awake, her voice whispered in the dark. "Quickly, we must leave this place."

For two nights, Eric and Cateline had stayed at the orphanage ran by the Monks of St Saxxa.

"What—"

"Sush! Come with me. Wrap that sack around you."

Eric wrapped the cornsack that served as a blanket around his shoulders. Cateline led him out the door and down the darkened stairs, across the courtyard to a corner in the fence.

"Quickly—through here." She squeezed through a hole in the broken, wrought iron and pulled Eric behind her.

"Cateline, why are we leaving?"

"There are evil people in there, Eric. You must trust me; Mother and Father would never have allowed such people near us."

"I want Mother." The mention of his mother brought a flood of tears. "I want to go home!"

"Quickly! We must find somewhere to hide." She grasped his arm and they ran down the hill towards the waterfront.

Three years older, Cateline was his only remaining family. In his five years of life, Eric had always had the security of two parents and his sister.

"I'm sorry, Eric." Cateline's voice shook as they ran through the shadows, every few steps she looked back. "Mother and Father are both gone. It's just you and me now, we must be brave. I'll do my best to care for you."

Eric sobbed as he ran reliving the flames, screams, buckets of water, and running feet—strange men carrying them through the smoke. The night that took his home and parents would live forever in his memory.

Cateline led Eric to the waterfront markets and they curled up, out of the wind between two stalls. They slept until daybreak when the merchants arrived with their hustle and bustle.

"Well hello, what have we here?" A woman's cheerful face peered into the gap where they had spent the night. Eric rubbed his eyes as Cateline got to her feet and smoothed her hair.

"We needed somewhere to sleep."

"Where are your parents?"

Sleep-befuddled, Eric rubbed his eyes.

*Where am I? Where is mother?*

"We don't have any parents."

Cateline's answer brought him fully awake.

"You poor little souls, come—I'll take you to the monastery. They'll take care of you."

"No, please! We just left there, they're bad people. We will not go back."

Eric thought Cateline sounded like their mother had, stern and decisive.

"You know," the woman squeezed her jowls between fingers and thumb, "I've heard that said before. Yes, I've heard that. I'd take you to my house but my daughter and all her little ones have moved in since her husband ran away to sea, so I have no room for you." She nodded and her muddy green eyes lit with inspiration. "Let me see if I can find you something to eat. Wait here—don't go away now will you?"

She waddled away and Eric gazed after her.

"I'm hungry, Cateline." A rumble from his stomach gave credence to his words. The tiny bowl of gruel the monks had fed him held little sustenance.

Cateline's arm around his shoulders comforted Eric and eased his fears. He had begun to think the woman had forgotten them when he saw her waddling back; another hungry growl gurgled below his ribs.

"Here we are, kiddies, an apple and a bun for each of you." She puffed to a halt. "The ladies at the charity shop down the other end said you must come to them and get some warm clothes. You can't be seen wandering the streets in hopsack. Old Basil from the city watch will take you for runaways."

"Thank you," said Cateline.

"Thanks—" The bun muffled Eric's voice; his stomach growled as his mouth took too long to send it down.

"My name is Marsie. What are your names?"

"Cateline and Eric."

"Such lovely names—you could be a princess with a name like Cateline. And Eric. I expect in the fullness of time your name shall be revered—for names are powerful things—yes!"

Eric glanced at Cateline's solemn face then returned his attention to the bun.

"Smile, kiddies!" Marsie ruffled Eric's hair. "Today is Coronation Day."

"What's a coronation?" Eric's words squeezed past a mouthful of bread.

"Today they are crowning our new King—such a handsome lad, Prince Raulin—just sixteen years old. We all trust our hopes to him. Well, I must be off, lots of work to do." Marsie waddled away, shaking her head. "A boy King! What next?"

**************

Ninety-five days after his crowning, Raulin passed stewardship to Reeve Calder, donned his battle regalia of chainmail and heavy leather armour.

Calder helped him with the buckles. "I'm not happy with allowing you to lead this mission, your Majesty."

"I have to show the people that I am not afraid to lead from the front. I cannot sit here in the safety of Castle Greycliff and expect my men to do my bidding."

"Raulin, you are sixteen years old. Even the squires are not sent into battle until they are seventeen."

"Fear not, Calder. Thirty of my knights, ten of the Elite Guard, and another sixty men will accompany me. I doubt we'll have to fight a major battle. The knights have located an encampment near the province of Redgraves. They think about fifty men; we can easily defeat them."

"You'd be better to observe them until you're certain they're enemies."

"We've had them under surveillance for a month. They are making weapons and their numbers have increased, Calder. We have to assume they mean us harm. If I allow their numbers to grow any further, we will have a major battle to fight."

"Well, take my advice at least, Raulin. Try to find out who is behind it. Peasants are not likely to decide to overthrow the King on a whim. It's highly likely to be a disenchanted aristocrat behind it."

"My father kept these people under control—while I've no wish to be the harsh ruler my father was I cannot be seen to be weak either."

At first light, Raulin and his men loped along Castlebridge Road. The early risers of King's Port cheered and wished them well. Raulin's eyes took in a little boy and girl among the waterfront merchants and wondered whom they were. He concluded them the children of a stallholder.

South from the city, they rode, and after midday, Sir Dowden guided his horse alongside Raulin's. "Your Highness, the scout, Vildar, tells me our quarry's encampment is over this rise."

"What is your advice, Sir Dowden?"

"We should stop here and send Vildar to assess their numbers."

Raulin nodded. Sir Dowden raised his arm and the company halted. "Take a rest, people. Vildar, you know the terrain. Scout ahead and report back inside the hour."

Vildar passed his spear to Sir Dowden and smiled. "Hold this for me, if I'm discovered I can't pretend to be a lost wayfarer while carrying the King's spear. I'll keep my sword." The scout took a lump of bread from his saddlebag, took a bite and nudged his horse to a trot. When the scout had disappeared over the rise, the men dismounted to eat, drink, and rest.

Vildar reappeared behind them some forty minutes later. Several of the men grabbed for their spears before they recognised their comrade.

"You gotta stop doing that, Vildar." One of the men allowed his spear to fall back into its holder. "You could die with a spear through your chest."

As nightfall loomed, Raulin led his men in a pincer attack; he and forty others charged with the sun at their backs. The surprised enemy scrambled for their weapons; many fled into the path of sixty soldiers who approached from the opposite direction.

"In the name of the King, lay down you weapons!" Sir Dowden thundered. "Surrender or die!"

Raulin hid his revulsion at having to kill but the undisciplined enemy fought savagely in the absence of their commander. The battle ended quickly; twenty men surrendered, the rest lay dead. Five of the King's men had died and as many wounded. Blood and guts freckled the combatants.

Back in King's Port, the knights spent days interrogating the prisoners.

"So none have volunteered the identity of their leader?" Raulin's eyes moved from man to man as they breasted the table in his war room.

"Not a word. In fact a couple of them have said they'd rather die than reveal their leader."

"How does one inspire such loyalty?"

Calder smiled. "Threaten them with an excruciating death, I imagine."

"What if I threaten them with the same?"

Sir Dowden smoothed his beard and sighed. "The fact that you didn't slaughter every last one of them at Redgraves told them you're not a violent man. They'll take their chances—the young King might behead them; their leader will most certainly see them die in lingering agony."

Calder sipped his wine and set the cup down. "So holding them isn't going to help."

"Set them free."

"Your Majesty? Why? It's clear they are part of plot against you."

"I want each of them followed. I want to know where they go and who they speak to."

"But—"

"If I kill them, I'll never know who they're working for. If I keep them locked up, it may take years before one of them cracks."

Calder smiled. "Good thinking, King Raulin. If they see you as a soft touch, they might become careless."

Sir Dowden studied the young monarch through narrowed eyes. "Your father would have their heads on spikes by now."

"It is my wish to redress my family's name. I want the people to know I care about their lives, that I care about their well-being. I don't believe this mission has ended the ambitions of those who would depose me, but I'm sure we have stalled their plans."

# 3

As the days turned to months, Eric and Cateline made the sheltered space between the stalls their home. Hunger, like a recurring drumbeat, ruled their lives. Their nights held many terrors as footsteps passed in the dark. By day, they wandered the waterfront. Sometimes they earned a penny sweeping for the stall owners. They dared not wander deeper into the city, which had vagrants and beggars on every corner.

"Young Eric." Wischard called from the front of his stall, the wrought iron Glaziers Guild sign over the door squeaked as it swung in the breeze. "Would you like to earn a penny?"

"Yes." Eric's stomach rumbled—he could feed himself and Cateline for two days with a penny.

"I need a strong lad to carry sand from the beach. My old knees are giving me bother and I can't walk the distance anymore."

Eric wore his own path to the beach as he trudged to and fro with buckets of sand for the glazier. As he scooped the sand into buckets, he gazed out to sea and wondered what lay beyond the horizon. Where the ruffled waters faded into the mist a line of islands broke through. One giant pillar of rock rose tall and narrow above the others.

*Someday I'm going to see those islands.*

Eric wondered if anyone lived there. A ship with sails aloft moved towards the tall rock. He grinned as a red dragon flapped lazily overhead across the city and vanished from view. What an awe-inspiring world it was.

With each trip, he rested and enjoyed the warmth of the glazier's furnace. He watched, enthralled as Wischard turned the sand to liquid and made a sheet of glass.

"That's like magic, Wischard."

The old man laughed. "It would be much easier if it was done with magic, Eric. Perhaps I should learn some."

"I'd like to do magic." Eric had never known how they made glass and it inspired him to keep a handful of sand in his pocket. With his penny, he bought a cob of bread to share with his sister. They still had a halfpenny left for the next day. Wischard said he would have more work for him later that week.

**************

One freezing night in the middle of winter, as Eric pulled his cornsack tighter and closed his eyes, Cateline spoke.

"Your birthday is somewhere about now. You're six years old. Mother said you were born on the winter solstice."

"What's a winter solstice?"

Cateline snuggled closer. "I don't know. Maybe when it gets coldest. Go to sleep now."

"I'm hungry."

"Your stomach is a bottomless pit, Eric."

**************

Eric awoke to a scream and a bad smell. Cold air rushed over him and a man's voice startled him to his feet.

"Well, look what I found." The odour of sweat and fish filled the space between the stalls. His sister punched and kicked; a man grasped her arm and dragged her to the sidewalk.

"That's right, darlin', Fight! I like a lass with sass."

He threw the little girl onto the cobblestones and knelt over her. Eric ran at the man and kicked his jaw. He quailed as the sneering face lifted towards him. The sand in his pocket bumped against his hip.

"You little—"

Eric snatched a handful of the sand and threw it in the man's eyes. Curses filled the marketplace as Eric pulled Cateline to her feet; they fled before the man regained his sight.

The children spent the night, huddled under a dragon statue in the town square. Only in the light of day, they dared return to the markets.

"Oh, thank heavens!" Eric welcomed Marsie's relieved cry, she and the charity shop women had befriended the children. "Where have you been?"

**************

That afternoon, Marsie took Cateline to Onfroi's manor; the wealthy merchant employed her as a kitchen maid, assistant to Elspeth, the cook.

"They don't pay much, dear." Elspeth took Cateline's hand and examined her palm. "But you will have a roof

15

over your head until your future beckons—and what a future it promises—"

"But what about Eric?"

Cateline's concern for him touched Eric. "I'll be okay, Sis. I can run awfully fast when I have to, and I can sleep down at the markets."

"I can't have him in the house, Mr Onfroi won't allow it." Elspeth checked behind her and learned down to whisper. "Wait until the grooms leave the stable each night, you can sleep up in the loft, but you must never allow anyone to see you in there, Onfroi is a cruel man."

Each night, Eric slept in the stable. He discovered he could, if needed, come and go without climbing the loft ladder. The hay door opened to a narrow ledge above the stable yard. Eric could walk along to the top of a high wall that separated the yard from Silversage Street. From there he could jump onto a neighbouring rooftop. Most nights, Cateline hid a small parcel of food behind the rain barrel outside the kitchen door, without which, Eric feared he would starve.

As Eric grew, so did his confidence. He didn't consider himself homeless, the streets were home and the stable loft his bed of straw. Working for Wischard, carrying sand and sweeping his floor, provided a small wage.

He learned to avoid Onfroi's teenaged son, Aldus, who swaggered around King's Port with a gang of sycophants intimidating the boys and girls of the city. Late one afternoon, Eric finished work at Wischard's and took a short cut through a winding lane; he found a boy surrounded by Aldus and his gang.

"Look lads—a street kid!" A malicious grin split Aldus's pimpled visage. "Been thieving haven't you gutter rat? Turn out your pockets!"

The boy tried to flee but one of Aldus's cohorts blocked his retreat, another kicked his skinny legs from under him and he dropped to the mud; the older boys jeered and laughed. The boy rose and swung punches but they pinned his arms behind his back while Aldus beat him.

"That's what happens to gutter rats who don't do as they're told!" Aldus syncopated his words with punches. Eric charged and pushed Aldus into a muddy puddle. Onfroi's son clambered upright, his face pale under a mask of mud and his fine clothes dripped with muck and horse dung. "You'll pay for that you—"

"Hail you! Who goes there?" A shout from the entrance to the laneway distracted Aldus and his friends; they scurried away. A stooped man in a top hat marched down the lane. "Are you hurt, lads?"

"We're fine." Eric helped the boy to his feet—his nose bled, his lip swelled and his eye promised a fine shade of purple by morning.

"Go to the wharf and wash those cuts in seawater." The man examined the boy's face. "Try to stay out of trouble in the future—old Basil hates kids." He walked off without a backward glance.

"I thought I was staying out of trouble."

"Let's get out of here." Eric drew the frightened boy out of the lane and onto Silversage Street. "What's your name? Where do you live?"

"I'm Yrian and I live down on the waterfront." The boy extended a muddy hand for Eric to shake.

"My name's Eric."

"Haven't I seen you carrying sand to Wischard's?"

"Yes, that's me."
"Where do you live?"
"Nowhere."

# 4

Castle Greycliff reared high above the city and the breakwater at the entrance of King's Port Harbour. At low tide the serpentine moat flowed from the open sea and circled the base of the fortress. At high tide, the torrent thundered; a perpetual rush of waves as they receded to expose the barnacled rocks—slither back to climb the weathered stones towards the battlements, crash and spray foam into the air. Across the centuries, the seabirds swooped and shrieked—the discordant sound of the city. Its folk would only notice if they fell silent.

The years rolled by uncounted. Eric outgrew his clothes before they wore out; he worked and avoided trouble. In his spare time, he roamed the city with Yrian—laughing and making crazy plans. Eric never knew his exact age; it seemed an eternity since his parents had died.

Each Wednesday, Cateline had an afternoon off. She met Eric in the town square, away from Aldus and his thugs' haunts.

"Cateline," Eric sat with his sister, gazing at pigeon droppings on a statue. "How old am I?"

"I don't know exactly, but I think you're nearly thirteen years old—because I'm sixteen. There have been so many winters and you're nearly as tall as me."

"Do you think I'll grow much taller?"

"I'm sure you will, you—"

A group of riders rattled across the castle bridge, three lines of ten led by a flagbearer, the black and grey pennant flapped in the wind. Spears and pikes pointed to the clouds as they cantered along Castlebridge Road and disappeared into the city.

Eric stared. "Do you think they're going to fight a war?"

"I don't know. They had spears and swords."

"One day I might be a soldier."

"It's not what mother and father would have wished for you, Eric."

A pair of red dragons flew overhead and glided to the cobblestones in front of the Coliseum, the enormous stadium stood in the shadows of Castle Greycliff. Their riders slid from their shoulders and led the beasts around the side of the building.

Eric smiled. "Perhaps I'll ride a dragon."

Cateline laughed. "Perhaps."

That night as he lie in the hay and listened to the cribber, chewing the door of his stall, Eric gave more thought to his future. He wondered if he could get a job like those men on the horses. They worked for the King, the man who ruled Oldegoth and its people. Eric had never seen the King and imagined him to be a muscle bound giant with a sparkling golden crown on his head.

He speculated what his parents would have wanted for him. They had both worked for the fishmonger, scaling and gutting fish. In the winter, they came home with chaffed hands.

*Were you happy, Mother and Father?*

He vaguely remembered their faces, talking and laughing as they cooked and ate dinner. He smiled through his tears; well he remembered their bedtime stories and songs. He fell asleep with his mother's voice ringing in his memory.

Thoughts of his future returned the next day. Trip after trip, he strode into Wischard's Glaziers with a pail of sand in each hand. Though he carried the loads easier with each passing day, they still dragged on his shoulders and blistered his fingers.

"Good lad, Eric." Wischard smiled as he polished a sheet of glass. "How many pails have you carried today?"

"I don't know, sir."

"Haven't you been counting?"

"I don't know how, sir."

Wischard scanned Eric from head to his bare toes. "Well, we can't have that, lad. Come and have some bread and cheese and I'll teach you about numbers. Do you know how to write your name?"

"No."

"Come and sit down."

Eric followed as Wischard shuffled into the tiny kitchen at the back of his shop.

"Wischard, I saw some soldiers leaving the castle yesterday. Is there a war?"

"No, Eric. Soldiers are often sent out so that the people know the kingdom is being watched, to reassure the people and to deter insurgents."

"What are insurgents?"

"People who want to steal the King's crown—trouble makers."

"Are there any in Oldegoth?"

"Many like to believe there are none, but that is not true. There are rumours of a planned coup, but so far, they don't know who to arrest. All they have managed to do is delay what they think is the inevitable."

That night Eric made his way to Onfroi's manor where he hid in the alley until the grooms left, then slipped inside the stable. As he climbed the ladder to the loft, a groom returned unexpectedly. Startled, Eric clambered up the last rungs but he'd been discovered.

"Lord Onfroi! Come quickly—there is a thief in the stable!"

Eric escaped through the hay door, scrambled along the ledge to the wall and jumped onto a nearby rooftop. Concealed by a chimney, he watched another homeless boy, Jerrold, approach the front of the stable. Eric dared not shout a warning. Onfroi's men seized the boy and dragged him into the alley. From his hiding place, Eric peeped through his fingers as the men beat the little boy until his cries faded and died.

"Take him to the harbour and throw him in." Onfroi nudged the dead boy's undernourished body with his knobby cane. "I won't have vermin of any kind living in my stable."

Eric fled across the roofs, down a wall and away through the shadows. Out of the city, along a path lit by the flickering lighthouse, he shivered and wished for the warmth of his cornsack; a frigid wind whistled through the heather and froze his fingers, toes, and ears. He hunkered down to sleep but the howls of the freezing squalls kept him awake. When the early morning sky lightened, Eric rose and moved on. Across a wide pebbled beach, a rocky headland looked promising; he needed shelter. A small stream meandered down to the sea; he followed it towards its source through a jagged gap hidden in the hillside. The water chilled his bare feet as he paddled along the stream and into an immense cavern; the waterway flowed along one side. Eric climbed the rocks and discovered a hidden sandy ledge. Exhausted, he lay down to rest and woke hours later with a dry mouth and rumbling stomach. He climbed down and tested the water in the stream—cool and fresh. He ventured out of the cavern to a high tide; raging surf pounded the beach. Waves lapped the foot of the hill. He followed the stream to the tide line, chipped oysters off the rocks and ate ravenously. Feeling better for the food in his belly, he climbed back to the ledge and as he fell asleep, he smiled. He rather liked this new hidey-hole.

*Poor little Jerrold. I hope Onfroi pays for that murder.*

**************

As evening fell, Eric stole along Silversage Street to his hiding place in the shadows behind Onfroi's manor and waited. Well after dark, Cateline emerged from the backdoor and tipped scraps into the pig's bin.

"Psst!" Eric didn't dare call out.

Cateline searched the darkness. "Hello? Who's there?"

Eric moved but remained in the shadow. "It's me, Sis."

"Eric?"

"Over here!" He dare not move closer.

"Wait there!" She disappeared back into the house. Gone less than a minute, she re-emerged and crept across the cobblestones to where Eric hid. She threw her arms around him. "Oh Eric! I heard Onfroi talking to his men about a boy they killed. I worried it might be you; I've felt sick since I heard. Elspeth has been very upset too. You aren't the only boy we leave food out for."

"It was little Jerrold—they beat him to death, Cateline! There was nothing I could do."

"You must not blame yourself. Here." Cateline passed him a half loaf of bread. "It's all I could get."

"Thank you, Cateline, I'm hungry. Hey, don't worry if you don't see me for a few days, I have a new hiding spot along the coast past the lighthouse, but I will come back every few nights."

Voices and a rattling of crockery came from inside the manor house.

Cateline hugged him. "Go quickly, and be careful!"

She hurried to the back door and slipped inside.

# 5

The candles in the King's parlour burned down, the bottle of wine dipped low. Raulin and his closest friend, Larkin played chess and talked—a frequent pastime for the two since their boyhood. Larkin had watched and sympathised as Raulin interred his father and took the King's Oath. Young King Raulin solemnly swore to govern the Kingdom of Oldegoth with justice and mercy—something his father hadn't always done. Now twenty-four, Raulin had grown accustomed to the position.

Larkin manoeuvred his bishop two squares from Raulin's knight. "How was your meeting with the Slokks and Gigags?"

Raulin studied the board and wriggled his fingers over the head of his rook. "The Slokks were their usual cantankerous selves but the Gigags are happy to continue their patrols along the archipelago. Given half a chance, the Slokks would close the Dorcliff Channel but between our fleets and the Gigag's Dragon Knights I think we can rest assured the channel will remain open."

"My people will be pleased—if the Channel closed, their lives would become—"

Knuckles on the door broke their relaxed conversation.

"Come!"

The door swung inward and Raulin's aid and reeve, Calder, entered. "Good evening, your Majesty. Larkin," he saluted, "I trust you're well? Raulin, your brother, Prince Randolf would like a word."

"Send him in, and Calder—stay. I want you to hear what he has to say for himself."

"Certainly, Raulin."

Larkin rose.

"You don't have to go, Larkin. In fact I'd like you to stay too." Raulin waved him back to his chair. "Besides I haven't finished beating you off the board yet."

"And you never will."

"Stay. I need others to witness my brother's excuses."

Larkin resumed his seat, picked up his wine, and flung a leg over the arm of the chair.

Raulin turned in his chair as Randolf entered. "Good evening, Randolf. You have some news for me?"

Randolf smirked and bowed.

Raulin sighed. "No need to bend your spine, little brother—I'm well aware of its pliability."

Randolf's eyes narrowed. "You asked me to report Lord Onfroi's activities, Sire—though you're yet to sire anything."

"I'm sure a suitable wife is somewhere out there waiting for me to sweep her off her dainty feet, but you needn't concern yourself with my private life, Prince Randolf."

"Lord Onfroi—"

"Onfroi is not a Lord, Randolf, as much as he wants to be. Now do tell, what is the commoner, Onfroi, up to?"

"He has suggested his niece, Lady Cassandra, would make a suitable wife for myself."

Raulin glanced at Larkin who fidgeted and scratched his nose. "Yes, I believe he has put her forward to every eligible aristocrat in the kingdom—I will approve the marriage when the Lady Cassandra is of beddable age. What else have you to tell? Are my informants correct when they say Onfroi is agitating for a dethroning?"

"I don't believe so." Randolf's eyelids fluttered, his attention flicked from Raulin to Calder to Larkin and then dipped to the floor. "I have not seen nor heard anything to suggest your sovereignty is in danger. Sire."

Raulin eased himself from his chair and towered over Randolf.

"If you want to keep that fat head on your shoulders, little brother, bite your weasel's tongue and remember to whom it is you're speaking."

"Yes, your Majesty."

"Dismissed, Prince Randolf."

Randolf turned on his heel and strode from the room.

Larkin gazed at the closed door. "Would you really have his head?"

Raulin exhaled long and loud. "No. I doubt I'll ever order anyone beheaded—that was my father's specialty. I am not my father."

"I am glad to hear that."

# 6

As happened every Saturday afternoon, Dragon screams from the King's Port Coliseum overwhelmed the bonhomie of their handlers as they prepared for the tournament. Outside, people jostled and queued for the best seats; nobody wanted a ringside seat, where you had a good chance of being fried to a crisp. Eric and Yrian padded barefoot along the waterfront on Castlebridge Road, eager to watch the dragon tournament. King Raulin the Redeemer granted free entry to the Coliseum on odd occasions and thousands attended. They sang and waved homemade flags in anticipation of a rare treat.

"Fresh and sweet! Toffee apples!" The hawker's spiel echoed from somewhere ahead. "Three for a penny!"

The proximity of food inflamed his hunger, but Eric's penniless status left him wanting. He hoped Cateline would leave some food out for him that night. The boys climbed Castlebridge Road to join the excited townsfolk in the square. Acrid sweat mingled with the aroma of fish and fresh bread drifting from the waterfront markets.

"Make way for the King's Men!" At the cry, the crowd split down the middle and pressed against the walls. A troop of mounted soldiers trotted through; in their midst, a man sat astride a horse, his hands tied behind him. As they passed, people laughed, some jeered and threw apple cores at the prisoner—all a part of a fine afternoon's entertainment. When the horses had moved on, they resumed their trek to the coliseum, many speculated on why the king's men had arrested someone.

Yrian quickly lost interest in the prisoner. "Who will you cheer today?" He shouted over the hubbub. His voice cracked.

"The same as always—Larkin on Telzoth the Magnificent." Eric shouldered his way past a group of dawdlers.

"Me too! Larkin's the greatest Dragon Ace in the whole Kingdom."

"Let's get a ring side seat so we can see them up close."

"Yeah let's! I'm not afraid to sit close to the dragons."

Eric led Yrian to front seats halfway along the straight and they waited. Though a common sight over King's Port, Eric had rarely seen a dragon up close. He and Yrian cowered as a black dragon passed, fast and low, the draft from its wing buffeted their ears. It screeched, shot flames and flew up to circle the top of the Coliseum.

"Woah!" Yrian's face turned from white to red.

Eric swallowed the hysterical laughter that bubbled in his chest, his heart banged against his ribs. He gulped like a fish pulled out of the bay.

Yrian quailed as another dragon soared past, its wings wafted grit in their faces. "Do you think we should move to a safer seat?"

"Maybe—no—I don't want to miss anything, do you?"

"No, let's stay here!" Yrian's voice piped through the cheers of the crowd. "I'm going to become a dragon ace when I grow up."

"Me too!"

For hours, the dragon aces guided their mounts through hoops, between upright poles and under low bars. They grabbed banners as they flew past and dropped them into a basket. With each low pass, the crowd leaned back in their seats. The speed and accuracy of the dragon aces as they raced around the ring enthralled Eric, and he fantasised about a day he too owned a dragon.

**************

The Reeve of King's Port nodded and the King's first knight led the prisoner away to the dungeons.

"Do you think it's worth holding him, Calder?" King Raulin leaned against the wall and gazed after Cesper and the prisoner.

"Probably not, but holding him might make his cohorts stop and think. Young Sir Cesper will arrange for a couple of squires to follow him when he's released."

Raulin sighed and rubbed his eyes. This had been a long session; the prisoner had told them nothing they didn't already know—and they knew frustratingly little. "The knights think I'm weak because I won't rack him."

"Perhaps we could apply some pain for his next session."

Raulin grimaced. "Next session? Do you really think he knows anything?" For eight years, Raulin and his knights had worked to expose the man inspiring the rumours of a coup. His continued sorties into the provinces had so far kept his enemies at bay.

"Well he was certainly in the right place at the right time, your Majesty."

"Very well. We'll give him a night in the darkest dungeon and try again."

"Using force?"

"Let me think it over."

# 7

Hann scowled. The kid following him had begun to ask questions at the foot of Cradletop Mountain—the tallest mountain on Dorcliff Island. Now half way to the top, Hann needed his lungs for breathing, answering questions might kill him. The other three men in his party puffed and cursed as they lagged behind.

"Dragons have four legs, so how come the Golden Wyvern only has two legs?"

"Because he asked too many questions and got the others bitten off."

Fifteen-year-old Balien chortled like a guinea pig. "Naw!"

"It's because he's a Wyvern. They're different to dragons. They only have two legs and they don't spit fire; they spit acid. They're much more savage than a dragon."

"Are there many Wyverns on this island?"

"No, only Gernellian—the Golden Wyvern. The rest live on the Rock of Wycliff, that big rock that reaches the sky—we sailed past it this morning."

"Oh. Well how come Gernellian is the Emperor of Dorcliff."

"The old timers reckoned he was banished by his own kind. He got mixed up with some evil wizard or something like that—I don't know—stop talking and climb."

"And so he moved to Dorcliff and took over? What a mongrel!"

"I'm not complaining. He allows us all the eggs we want."

"That's not fair to the dragons."

"Not my worry—now shut up kid! Every dragon on Dorcliff Island will hear us." His nephew hadn't been nest raiding before and Hann secretly predicted the kid would wear his pants out sliding down the mountain to get away as soon as he sighted his first dragon.

"Hey, Uncle Hann, can I keep a couple of the eggs I raid?"

"No—I pay you a wage to collect them for me. Now hush or I'll wack you with my egg-pole."

Hann and his party stopped to rest, eye level to the dragon's sandy nesting ground. An old queen warmed the sand with a steady jet of flame; she would soon leave her nest to hunt. She buried her eggs; heatwaves distorted the air above her nest as she spread her leathery green wings and took to the sky. Hann and his men had limited time to gather the eggs and flee. The female dragons would return to the nest to consume their kill.

The hot sand could burn the inexperienced but the raiders carried an egg-pole—a long, hickory rod with a spoon-shaped paddle on one end. Hann carefully scraped away the sand, lifted the eggs separately from the nest and eased them into his fur-lined basket; his band of raiders repeated this process across the nesting sand. Other queens glared at the raiders from their nests, they hissed and bared their teeth but Hann knew they wouldn't interfere unless the raiders approached.

"Hurry, men!" he called, "We must be quick. These eggs cannot be allowed to cool or the young inside will die."

"Yeah—yeah, we know." The men guffawed and snorted; they had heard it before. "Most of them die anyway."

Only Balien cared enough to hurry; he spooned the eggs carefully and quickly.

Hann transferred the last egg to his basket. "Doesn't matter. My buyers still pay, while ever a few survive, they'll keep paying."

He refitted the lid to the basket and prepared to leave. A shadow fell upon him. The old, green queen loomed overhead, a dead deer clamped in her jaws. Her wings tossed sand to sting Hann's face; she dropped the carcass, schrieked and lunged. Hann fell on his back, swung the egg-pole and hit her across the face. She snarled, snapped her jaws, a shake of her huge head severed Hann's foot. All his party except Balien ran and left him to his fate.

"Quickly, Uncle Hann." The blast of flame singed Balien's hair as he dragged Hann across the sand and down the path. The dragon queen reared to strike again and a raucous hiss exploded from close by.

Hann looked back; Emperor Gernellian the Oppressor, the monstrous, golden Wyvern snarled over the twitching body of the dragon queen, a glob of noxious, yellow acid foamed and fumed. Her head dissolved in the Wyvern's caustic spittle. Gernellian hissed at the remaining queens; slimy ropes of viscous, yellow saliva swung from his jaws and dripped, fizzling into the sand. Hann watched in fear as his nephew ran back and grabbed the baskets. The Wyvern's maw yawned, black forked tongue curled over his snout to display the crimson acid ducts underneath. He hissed but didn't spit.

Hann laughed through his pain as Balien set the baskets down and stated the bleeding obvious.

"She bit your foot off!" He tore his tunic into strips and tied it over Hann's wound to stanch the blood flow.

Balien wanted to leave the eggs and support Hann back down the mountain.

"No, boy—you risked your life to retrieve them now carry them, I'll manage."

Balien hesitated. "We can get more eggs some other time."

"Dragons only nest once a year and those eggs are worth ten pound each."

"How much is ten pound?"

"Well, I pay you four shillings for this whole trip, right?"

"Yeah."

"Well, if four shillings is this much," Hann held up his finger and thumb, "then ten pounds is this much." He spread his arms and staggered.

"Careful, Uncle. Alright, I'll carry them."

As they made their way down the mountain, Hann distracted himself from his pain by asking Balien questions. "What are you going to do when you get older?"

"I want to breed dragons."

"Yeah?"

"I'll be the richest man in Oldegoth."

"Hm. Do you have a young lady, Balien?"

The boy's face glowed. "Naw!"

"Good! Keep it that way."

"Do you have a wife, Uncle?"

"I used to. Lucretia was her name, but she left me."

"I'm sorry."

"Don't be, I wasn't."

"Where is she now?"

"She's a dragon ace, rides in the King's Port Coliseum."

"Really? Does she own a dragon?"

"Hm. Sour natured, evil, gang-toothed monster. Her dragon's not very nice either."

Balien guinea-pig-chortled again.

Back on the boat, his nephew helped Hann to the captain's chair and fussed over him. His sister's boy had proven his worth on his very first egg-raid.

"How many eggs did you collect, Balien?"

"Ten. Now put your foot—shinbone—on this stool—Uncle—that's it, that will help stop the bleeding."

"Thanks, boy. They're yours—those eggs. Use them as your future breeding stock, but don't tell the other three."

"Thank you, Uncle Hann! Thank you!" Balien grinned all the way back to Oldegoth.

***************

At twenty-four years old, Raulin might well have been a hundred. Milo and Calder knelt on the filthy dungeon floor; lanterns surrounded the lifeless prisoner. Inch by inch they checked the dead man, searching for a cause of death. It irked Raulin that they'd found this perfectly healthy young man dead of no apparent cause. Judging by the marks on the dirty floor and his pain-wracked expression, he had died in agony.

"Here! I think I've found something—" Milo moved a lantern closer.

"What is it?"

"A tiny wound on his wrist."

"Perhaps it's just an insect bite."

"No. Look at the colouring. The surrounding skin is yellow."

"You don't suppose—no. It can't be."

Raulin stepped closer. "What do you think it is, Milo?"

"He's been imbued with wyvern toxin. It's a painful way to die."

Calder peered over his spectacles. "Perhaps they didn't intend to kill him. Perhaps the toxin was taken from a wyvern hatchling."

Raulin frowned. "Do you think the killer intended to create a Wrigon-norce?"

"Perhaps."

"Who would do that?"

"I know not, your Majesty. But if our diagnosis is true, we have a potential traitor in our midst. A dangerous traitor."

# 8

Another dragon tournament ended; Eric and Yrian sat on the breakwater and discussed the tactics each dragon ace used. For hours, they debated the finer points of dragon lore, and how much the skill of the ace contributed to the performance. They attended the Coliseum as often as they could afford it—Eric went without food to pay admission. The boys fancied themselves aficionados.

Yrian's eyes shone in the twilight. "We should each get a baby dragon, Eric."

"One day I will." Eric spoke the words but in his heart he saw little hope for a boy such as him to own a dragon.

The boys went their separate ways, Yrian to the little waterfront shack where his parents lived with seven hungry mouths to feed. Eric wandered the twists and turns of Silversage Street to Onfroi's manor. He stayed in the shadows and waited for the last window to turn dark, then waited some more. His stomach roiled loudly to remind him he had had no food since the night before. He crept over and found a bundle wrapped in muslin behind the rainbarrel.

*Thank you, Cateline—thank you.*

Eric earned enough for a little food but on Saturdays, he spent his money on admission to the Coliseum and depended on his sister's ability to pilfer scraps from Onfroi's table. Cateline had now worked in Onfroi's service for six years. Eric worried for her; at sixteen, men looked upon her as a woman. He dreamed of capturing a baby dragon and training it. If he could become a Dragon Ace, he could remove his sister from the danger of living under the roof of people who regarded her as property, of less importance than the horses in their stable. They paid her a pittance and made her work from dawn until the twilight faded.

Eric slunk back into the shadows and sat with his back against the wall. Potatoes, meat, and wrapped separately, a chunk of apple pie—a rare treat. He wolfed them; living on the streets had taught him to eat quickly. Taking time over a meal might see it snatched from under your nose. The food gone, Eric took a long drink from the rain barrel and shivered as the wind's icy fingers ruffled his hair. He had left it too late to go to his cave; the tide would be impassable and this wasn't a good night to sleep among the heather. He climbed up the wall, through the unlocked hay door and into Onfroi's stable loft. The horses nickered; the old cribber twitched his ears as he chewed on the door of his stall. Eric found the cornsacks that served as blankets and curled up.

**************

A loud click and a scrape of wood on stone woke Eric in the middle of the night. The door creaked open to men's voices. Curious, and fearful who could be down there at this hour of night, Eric crawled to the edge of the loft. He hid behind a bundle of straw and peered at the scene below. Onfroi held a lantern and a stranger backed a deep, mule-drawn cart into the stable. The mule snorted and tossed its head. The stabled horses nickered at the intrusion of a strange animal.

Onfroi poked his head out, looked both ways and closed the door. "How many did you get?"

"There's about forty—give or take." The stranger limped past the mule and pulled a cover from the cart to reveal deep straw. "Nearly got myself killed on this last trip. A big queen didn't want to part with her brood. She took my foot with her to her grave."

"You killed her?"

"No, Gernellian killed her."

"Killed by a wyvern, not a nice way to die."

"Yeah, he got her with a big glob of spit and we got away with a lot of eggs."

"What kind are they?"

"Mostly Common Dragons but there may be a few Parinith Dragons, we don't have time to check their talons, besides they've been interbreeding for so long, who can tell anymore?"

Eric's heart raced in step with his mind.

*Dragon eggs!*

He could see the man now; he had black hair, a long black beard and a thick moustache that covered his top lip. A wooden peg protruded from the leg of his breeches. He leaned on a long pole, with a spoon-shaped paddle at the top.

The peg-legged man stooped to peer into Onfroi's face. "You know Parinith Dragons are illegal here in King's Port? If one scratches you, you're dead."

Onfroi snorted. "Yes, our chicken-hearted monarch, Raulin the Redeemer, is afraid of their poisonous talons so he deprives us all of having real dragons."

"Down at Esterhaven they let you keep them. We coat their talons with soda-lime glass, it doesn't stop them from scratching but the poison doesn't get through." He pulled a large black egg out of the straw and handed it to Onfroi. "As I said, not all of them will hatch, in fact you'll probably only get eight or ten at the most but you'll get the dragons you're after—much cheaper than buying them as trained adults for around three hundred pounds each."

They moved the eggs to deep straw in the corner of the barn and covered them with cornsacks.

"I'll move them tomorrow to my warehouse down near the wharf—can't have fire breathing dragons in a stable full of straw." Onfroi chuckled, picked up the lantern and moved to the door. "How much do I owe you?"

Peg leg led the mule outside. Eric heard their voices fade as the door closed and the stable went dark.

# 9

Eric inhaled; his trembling hand wiped his brow. Wide-awake, he waited to see if anyone would return.

*Here is your chance, Eric—take it or regret it for the rest of your life.*

His earliest lessons in life taught him honesty but honesty would see him and his sister living as paupers for all their days. Owning a dragon would give him an opportunity for advancement. Finally, he came to a decision, grabbed his cornsack blanket and scrambled down to the floor. The cribber stopped chewing on his stall and stuck his head out for Eric to pat.

"I'm going to miss you chewing and snorting all night, but I won't be back again."

As he sorted through the eggs, he held one to his ear; soft croaking came from within. His hands shook as he selected five of the biggest, warmest, noisiest eggs and eased them into the jute bag with handfuls of straw. A snort from the old cribber behind him sent Eric's thudding heart crashing against his ribs. He rose on trembling legs, hefted the bundle over his shoulder and swayed under the weight. He cracked the stable door and peeped out, listening for the City Watch. He resisted the urge to run with his plunder.

He clung to the shadows and hurried along the street. Footsteps sounded in the night, Eric stepped into a dark alley, set the bag on the ground and waited. A bag of dragon eggs would raise some awkward questions; if anyone approached, he would disown them. The footsteps faded and Eric moved on. His stomach clenched; ahead he saw a tall, black-cloaked figure moving towards him. Again, he slipped into the shadows and watched the man hurry past; he vaulted the fence of the monastery and vanished behind a building. Eric crept towards the wharves and turned out of the city, along the misty coastline through the dark, the flickering lighthouse lit his way. The early morning's twilight lightened as he traversed the pebbled beach; the receding tide lapped his ankles. He navigated the rocky headland to his cavern and hefted the precious burden to his ledge. He found his kindling, lit a small fire and lay the eggs on straw in the sand. He hurried to a nearby dune for driftwood and dry grass.

**************

Eric worked at Wischard's each day, but didn't linger to chat. He hurried home to stoke the fire and turn the eggs, striving to keep them evenly warm. He talked to them and listened to the sounds within. One of the eggs fell silent and another lukewarm so Eric slept with it tucked in his shirt. He caught fish and collected eggs from the seabirds that nested further along the cove. He ventured up onto the headland to pick berries.

Each day he gathered seaweed and driftwood from the tide-line. After a summer storm, some useful things washed up on the beach: a couple of wooden crates, ropes, and an old fishing net. Eric carried them all back to his cave.

Cosy by the fired, Eric dozed after a large meal of fish, bird eggs and seaweed; a sudden crack startled him awake. The sound came from one of the eggs. Eric trembled and waited for hours before another crack split the circumference of the shell. Eric whooped as a wrinkled baby dragon tumbled onto the sand. It raised its head on a wobbly neck, emitted a tiny puff of smoke and rolled on to its back. Eric minded its talons as he set it upright and brushed sand off its scales. As big as the stray cats that roamed King's Port the baby dragon's wings spread almost as wide as Eric was tall. It had greyish blue eyes and the iridescent blue scales flashed gold in the firelight. He offered a piece of leftover fish to the little dragon; it sniffed and puffed more smoke followed by a short burst of flame. Eric dropped the fish and the hatchling snatched it, flipped it overhead, caught and wolfed it down. It sniffed around.

"Hungry are you?" The little dragon answered with a plaintive whine.

Eric fed it all his leftovers, then went down to the stream and speared another fish. While he fed the hatchling another egg cracked; Eric hurried away to catch more fish and returned as the second hatchling emerged.

The baby dragons ate their fill and hissed smoke at each other; eventually they curled up together and went to sleep. Eric closely examined them and concluded the blue dragon was female; she didn't have a spur higher up the inside of each leg. Eric called the first hatchling Azuria and the second, a male, he named Isuthiel, the name of a legendary dragon he remembered from a story told by one of the hazy figures that had been his parents. Isuthiel had silvery-green scales and the same greyish blue eyes as Azuria, though after a few hours their eyes turned emerald green.

# 10

The hatchlings' hungry squawks woke him at daybreak. He hastened to the stream, caught two fish, and collected a dish of oysters. He fed the dragons and cooked breakfast for himself. The hatchlings flapped wings but didn't attempt to fly. They liked to have their heads rubbed and he spent a lot of time petting and talking to them, hoping to make them easier to handle as they grew.

While Eric fed the baby dragons, Isuthiel grabbed at the fish and caught Eric's hand with his talons; Eric had never suffered such pain. He hurried down to the stream and washed it with fresh water but the stinging increased. As Eric returned to the ledge, his toes and fingertips tingled, his lips numbed and his body alternated hot and cold. Ringing in his ears increased, pulsed, and throbbed with his erratic heartbeat. One minute weak, his muscles contracted violently, Eric worried they might tear apart; his throat constricted painfully.

*This is where you die, Eric.*

He feared his sister would spend the rest of her life wondering what had happened to him. Blackness fell, the world faded out of time and matter. He floated, blinded by glaring light; buzzing filled his head. Things moved, thread-like figures he could not grasp in the indigo void—then black, nothing but black. Peace descended. A new existence came from the void; his sense of being, waxed and waned.

*'Thirsty,'* someone whimpered—*'I'm so thirsty. Water—must have water.'*

Something cracked in the miasma of his feeble existence and Eric woke. It could have been minutes; it could have been days. The pile of cold ashes where the fire had blazed told him it had been days. He staggered to his feet, Azuria and Isuthiel sat together in the sand watching him; beside them the cleanly picked bones of some creature. Eric swayed dizzily as he climbed down to the stream, drank and vomited. He sat in the water; its cooling effect soothed the fever. He submerged himself, surfaced and drank again; this time the water stayed down. A little better, he climbed back to his ledge. He looked again at the skeleton in the sand and searched for the egg he'd slept with in his shirt, only an empty shell remained. Azuria and Isuthiel had eaten the third hatchling. He lifted the straw where the last viable egg rested. Still warm and cracked, ready to hatch. As fast as his frail body permitted, he hastened to the stream to spear some fish and returned with five of good size. Eric didn't want the hatchlings hungry when the last emerged. He fed two each of the biggest fish to the dragons and cooked the last for himself. A few mouthfuls and the nausea returned. He whipped around as a croak reached his ears. A little black dragon wriggled in the sand—the back half still in the egg.

"You're late, and it's lucky you are or you might have been on the menu too."

The third hatchling was male and Eric named him Tenebrozi after the historically famous dragon he'd heard mentioned at the Dragon Coliseum. Unable to keep up the supply of fish to the babies he took the fishing net he'd scrounged from the sea after a storm and used it to catch seagulls which the hatchlings devoured, feathers and all. Eric received another scratch, this time from Tenebrozi and suffered no ill effects. Another long scratch from Isuthiel made Eric's head reel pleasantly but he did not lose consciousness. He noted Isuthiel's talons were sharp and black; the others' were short and pale. Curiosity compelled him to experiment. He had no reaction other than soreness from scratches by either Tenebrozi or Azuria, though for the third time, a scratch from Isuthiel left him happily detached, his muscles warm and relaxed. A quick experiment on a cave rat proved only Isuthiel was a Parinith Dragon—the kind the black bearded man mentioned.

*I thought a Parinith scratch was fatal. How am I alive?*

That year flew past. Each morning he took the baby dragons to the beach and watched them play. They became efficient hunters, snatching fish from the sea and birds from the air. He began training the dragons when they reached sheep size and still too small to ride. He accustomed them to wearing a rough harness he made from the ropes scrounged from the tide. He taught them to return to the cave when he whistled. He began riding them when they grew to horse size.

Between work and the dragons, Eric kept busy; Cateline, Yrian, and Wischard the only people with whom he had regular contact. Fearful he broke the law, he kept the dragons a secret.

When he knocked his head on a branch across the path he followed back to King's Port, Eric realized he had grown taller—taller in fact, than most of the men in King's Port. He received many more scratches from Isuthiel with no ill effects, he grew stronger and developed cat-like reflexes, his senses grew keener.

# 11

One stormy night in the middle of summer, Eric lay awake as lightning flashed through his cave entrance. He contemplated his next move. The dragon's second birthday approached and they had grown to double a horse's size. Impatient to compete in the Coliseum, Eric needed money to buy a decent harness and saddle. By morning, he'd reached a decision but first he must consult Wischard.

Wischard straightened from his work and raised his shaggy eyebrows. He leaned back and winced, trying to ease the stiffness in his spine.

"Esterhaven?"

"Yes, I need to go there." Eric tipped the last two pails of sand into Wischard's sand bin and hoped he didn't sound shifty.

"It's about thirty miles east along the coast—as the crow flies. You be careful down that way boy, they ain't all as friendly as the folk up here."

"I will be."

*How much worse than the most obnoxious inhabitants of King's Port can they be?*

"I'll see you in a few days."

He left before Wischard could ask questions. Hastening back to his cave he put the homemade rope harness on Isuthiel then prepared to mount.

"Don't look at me like that!" Azuria and Tenebrozi waited expectantly. "I'll be back before you know it."

With enough fish and seagulls to last them a day, he gave Azuria and Tenebrozi a long drink at the stream and tethered them inside the cave.

In Esterhaven, they landed before a stone building with a dragon statue in front and a wrought iron Guild of Dragon Merchants sign hanging from the façade. He led Isuthiel through the doors, a man dressed in a black coat and top hat, approached.

He bared yellow teeth and kneaded his palms. "What can I do for you, young sir? My name is Blazh." He proffered a hand and Eric shook it.

"I would like to sell this dragon but that reprobate across town only offered me two-hundred pounds." Eric set his brow with an indignant crease and hoped he sounded conversant in the value of dragons. He remembered the egg raider telling Onfroi the value of a trained dragon.

"Did he indeed?" Blazh's face grew inscrutable. "Let me look at him." He walked around Isuthiel who watched him nervously. Eric clutched the rope; it would not do for Isuthiel to singe the buyer's coat or eat his hat. "My! He is a fine specimen! How old is he?"

"Almost two so he has some growing to do yet. He's a Parinith Dragon from Dorcliff Island, well trained and very friendly." He smiled as Blazh give wide berth to Isuthiel's head and talons.

Blazh kept his face bland. "Indeed. Indeed. I can offer you two-hundred and twenty for him."

Eric remained silent though he wanted to jump in the air and whoop.

Blazh took his silence for hesitation. "Alright! Two-hundred and thirty then. I can't offer you any more, he is only a young beast and I have to feed him until sale day."

"Done!" Eric shook Blazh's hand and hid his elation. Two-hundred and thirty pounds was a vast fortune to a boy who'd never had any more than a few pennies in his pockets.

Blazh showed Eric where to leave Isuthiel. He patted the dragon's head and regretted his need to sell him but saw no alternative.

"You'll be alright, Isuthiel." Eric's eyes glazed as he scratched the dragon's head.

Blazh returned with a tin box. He counted the money into a leather pouch and passed it to Eric.

"Be very careful who you show that money to, boy, there are those who would cut your throat for it."

"Thank you, Blazh. I hope you find a worthy buyer for Isuthiel."

Eric went to the Coach Company and bought a ticket home to King's Port. Then he went to a pub called The Dragon's Claw and bought a dish of stew with bread, and a pint of ale. While he ate, a man with a black beard entered. He leaned on a pole and limped to a table across the small, gloomy barroom where sat another bearded man. The peg leg man flopped onto a chair and sighed.

"Noll, old chap! Good to see you again." He snapped his fingers at the barmaid. "Pint here please, Love?"

"Hann! I ain't seen you roun' for a few months, whaddaya been up to."

"Been up at King's Port, Onfroi's lookin' for men and I been tryin' to find them for him. Ta love." He took the pint from the barmaid and slurped. He palmed the froth from his moustache and rubbed it on his trousers. Eric ate, feigning deafness but the name Onfroi had drawn his attention.

A cigarette dangled from the corner of Noll's mouth; Eric saw him squint as the smoke stung his eye.

"Wos 'e want men for then?"

Eric barely heard Hann whisper. "Putting an army together; thinks he can overthrow the King."

"Geddowda here! Really?" Noll sat back in his chair, the cigarette ash fell into his ale.

"Shhh!" Hann looked around.

Ears alert, Eric scraped his plate and shovelled the stew into his mouth.

Hann chuckled. "Yeah! Silly twat! I'll take his money; he seems to have far too much."

Eric finished, thanked the barmaid and left. Waiting at the Coach Depot, he pondered what he'd heard in The Dragon's Claw.

*What would that mean for King's Port? What would it mean for Cateline if Onfroi tried to overthrow the King?*

He must get Cateline out of Onfroi's kitchen at the first opportunity.

*************

Eric arrived back at his cave in the early hours. He put a little of the money in his pocket and buried the rest in a dark corner.

Later that morning at the saddler's, Eric bought a new saddle and harness. He splurged on some new clothes and boots for himself; he had outgrown the few garments he owned. He took a walk to the waterfront markets and found Marsie, his childhood benefactor.

"Eric!" Marsie hugged his middle and stepped back. "My! Haven't you grown! You're becoming a handsome young man!"

Eric squirmed. "Marsie, I wonder if you can help me. I want to buy my sister a new dress but I don't even know where to go."

"Well isn't that perfectly charming of you, to think of your sister. Come on, I'll take you to the Emporium."

Eric chose two dresses for his sister and hoped she'd like them.

"Do you think she will like the colours?" Eric knew nothing of women's clothing and valued Marsie's opinion.

"Of course! They'll look lovely against Cateline's ivory complexion and dark hair."

**************

Eric met Cateline in the town square next to the Castle Bridge. In the shadow of Castle Greycliff, he waited impatiently for her to appear, eager to give her the dresses he'd bought.

"Finally!" he exclaimed as she walked across the stones towards him. He hugged her and ushered her over to where he had hidden a package. "I have something for you." He sat her down on the bench and pulled out the package.

"Eric!" She looked stern, "What is this?"

"Open it!" he insisted, grinning.

She peered into the package as though fearing a sharp-toothed creature dwelled within. She touched the folds of the blue dress and jerked her hand out.

"Where did you get it Eric?" she hissed, looking around fearing someone watched, "what have you been doing?"

Crestfallen at his sister's reaction, Eric looked around them. Nobody listened. "Well, it's like this…" The time had come; he had to tell her the whole story. "…and that's the truth. I know I shouldn't have stolen the eggs from Onfroi but—well—there were so many, I doubt he missed the few that I took. The dragons I still have are legal. I have enough money to tide us over until I can get established as a Dragon Ace. You can leave Onfroi's service any time you want."

Cateline's face relaxed and she smiled. "I don't know, I'll think about it. Thank you for the dresses, I won't get many opportunities to wear them but they're lovely."

Eric wanted to tell his sister what he'd heard at Esterhaven but didn't know how to broach the subject. Cateline, at eighteen, had few opportunities for work.

# 12

Helped by the luxury of a new saddle, Eric refined his riding skills as he trained Azuria and Tenebrozi. Tenebrozi was bigger and faster than Azuria but not as disciplined. Eric found him harder to control and had difficulty staying seated when the dragon turned sharply. Thrilling to ride, Tenebrozi's sinewy strength rippled under the shining black scales as he manoeuvred—diving fast and rising—his dark wings beat with prodigious strength. Though not as fast, Azuria's intelligence and tractability made her an easier ride, she responded to Eric's commands without hesitation. Eric decided he'd take her to the Coliseum first.

"You'll probably tip me off just when all the girls are watching." He patted Tenebrozi's neck. "We'll keep practicing though."

The black dragon puffed a thin jet of smoke, his sign of contentment.

***************

On Saturday morning, Eric rose early, donned his new outfit and boots; he polished Azuria's scales until she gleamed iridescent. He put on the harness and saddle.

"Wish us luck." He gave Tenebrozi a parting pat and climbed into the saddle. Tenebrozi sat down to eat the dish of apples Eric left him.

Eric landed on the street outside the dragon stables at the back of the Coliseum. He led Azuria through the big wooden doors that stood open, ready for the Dragon Aces' arrival.

"Who are you?" A rude demand greeted Eric, an attendant a couple of years older than Eric sat inside a small reception booth. "Who'd you steal the dragon from young fella?"

"She's mine." Eric worried if showing up unannounced was the right thing to do.

"I've never seen you before—or the dragon." He stepped out of the booth and scrutinised Eric from feet to face. "Wait there." He turned on his heel and strutted away, along the street and around the corner. Eric waited, wondering where he went and why he was so unfriendly. Minutes ticked by.

"Well, hello there!"

A fair-haired man approached. Eric recognized Dragon Ace, Larkin. Up close he looked younger than he previously thought.

"Hello." Eric opened his mouth to ask where he could register for the games when heavy footsteps approached.

"Hand me those reins, boy! You're under arrest for dragon theft." The red-faced man wore a black tunic with a circular badge on the front.

"I didn't steal it."

"One moment, Basil, you cannot be serious; you have proof of this charge, do you?" Larkin stood beside Eric, his brown eyes narrowed. Eric detected a faint accent. He'd heard sailors with that accent down at the wharves.

"No need for you to get involved, Larkin!" Basil grabbed Azuria's reins. "Young Wilmot has reported a crime and as head of the City Watch, I'm here to arrest a thief."

Azuria whipped the reins out of the officer's hand and Eric whistled the command to fly home. As she flew through the door, Azuria's wings knocked Wilmot on his rump and slapped Basil's face; she vanished into the morning sky. Basil chained Eric's hands, shoved him out the door and into the street. Wilmot scrambled to his feet and a satisfied sneer split his pimpled face.

"Out of the way, young Balien!" Basil snarled at a youth leading a red dragon along the street.

Balien stared and his dragon hissed.

# 13

The elderly Turnkey pushed the barred cell open, Basil shoved Eric and he tripped. The hard floor cut his cheek.

"Now Basil," the turnkey eased his speech, "there's nothing to be gained by injuring the boy."

"Shut up and do your job." The head of the City Watch strode away. "I'll be back for a guilty plea shortly; I'll get Wilmot's testimony first."

The turnkey helped Eric to his feet and removed the chains from his hands; he peered at Eric's face. "You alright, boy?"

"Yes—no!" Eric's head spun from the heavy fall. "That dragon is mine. I don't know why they think I stole it."

"Young kid like you? That's the first assumption they'd make. Wilmot is as foolish as his Uncle Basil."

Shouts reached them from the front of the Gaol house.

"What are they yelling about?" The Turnkey frowned, "Man can't get any peace around here with these hot tempered boneheads. My names Giles boy, what do I call you?"

"Eric." Eric's mind raced. "How can I get them to listen to me?"

"You won't, son." He cocked an ear to the shouts. "I'm just going to see what the ruckus is about." As if by magic, the cell gate swung closed and clicked as Giles walked away. He returned a minute later with a grin plastered on his face. "It would seem you have a powerful friend, Eric."

"I do?"

"Larkin, Dragon Ace, is off to get his lawyer." Giles's mouth twitched. "Basil is not pleased."

"Larkin?" Eric wondered if Larkin's lawyer would help him, and in this cold hard city—why would such people care?

He waited alone for hours; he heard the noise of the excited crowd and dragons coming from the Coliseum close by. The sky through the high barred windows turned from blue to pink; the clouds turned golden as the afternoon wore in to evening. He paced back and forth; worry gnawed his insides.

*What if they keep me here for weeks? What will happen to my dragons?*

The outer door opened and Giles returned; the cell gate clicked open as he approached.

"Come, laddie."

Eric followed him to the office. Basil's malevolent eyes gleamed. A beefy man with shaggy hair slapped a piece of parchment on the desk between them.

"Sign here, please."

"This is interference in my position as the head of the City Watch."

"Reeve Calder and the King have a hearing first thing Monday morning—do you want to take it before them?"

"We all know who the King is friendly with." Basil glowered and scribbled his name at the bottom of the page. The man passed the quill to Eric. Giles grinned as he shook Eric's hand and wished him luck with his dragon.

The lawyer strode to the door and beckoned Eric to follow.

"My name's Humphrey." He shook Eric's hand. "My client, Larkin, has asked me to take you to his house; he'd like a word."

Humphrey showed Eric to his carriage. They rode around the corner past the now silent Coliseum, his pony's feet echoed in the darkness. Around the edge of Castle Greycliff's mote, onto Castlebridge Road and out of the city; the road climbed steadily until they turned onto a narrow gravel road, through wrought iron gates.

"This is Mistmere, Larkin's manor." Humphrey hauled on the reins and halted in front of a manor high on a bluff with a view of the open sea far below.

"Humphrey, come on in!" Larkin flung the door wide. "And welcome to you, young Dragon Ace."

"His name is Eric." Humphrey drew him forward. "Eric, this is Larkin, the man who sent me to free you."

"I'm honoured to meet you, sir. Thank you for getting me out of there. I promise that dragon is mine."

"We worked that out easily," Larkin smiled. "Nobody has reported a dragon stolen for many years. Basil is too lazy to check before he arrests someone, he's too busy lining his own pockets."

Humphrey tied his pony to the hitching post. "I have a suspicion Basil might have been looking to secure a valuable dragon."

"I was thinking the same." Larkin examined the cut on Eric's cheek and shook his head. "Old Bas just had to get rough didn't he? I shall get Milo to dress it for you, yes?"

"No, don't worry." Eric's fingers found the cut and he winced, "it'll be fine."

Larkin led them into a luxurious parlour and invited them to sit. Eric had never been inside such a splendid house and tried not to gape.

"I'm afraid I can't offer you much in the way of good food, it's just bread and cheese until I can find another cook and housekeeper." He indicated for them to sit, and disappeared through a door at the other end of the room. He returned a short time later bearing a wooden tray with three large mugs of ale, and a marble platter of bread, cheese and thick slices of ham.

"My housekeeper left me yesterday—said she was getting married—bless her." He took a mug of ale and sat it on the little table beside Eric's chair along with the food. "So tell me about that lovely blue queen of yours."

"Queen?"

"Your dragon, she's a girl—is she not?"

"Yes, she is."

"You've not dealt with dragons for long, have you?"

"Um, a couple of years—since I hatched them—" Eric stopped, he worried he may have broken the law by hatching the dragons without a permit or something.

"We dragon aficionados call the females queens."

"Oh, I didn't know that."

They talked for hours; Eric told them about himself, though he left out how he acquired the dragon eggs and that Isuthiel had been a Parinith Dragon.

"You live in a cave? This is fascinating! When you get to be a champion Dragon Ace you can buy yourself a nice house like this, yes?" He splayed his hands at his surroundings.

Eric asked the question that had played on his mind all afternoon. "Did I do the wrong thing just showing up at the Coliseum today?"

"No, not at all. Such a pity the first person you ran across was Wilmot. He would have taken one look at a handsome young chappie like you and well— you saw what happened, no? He's a spiteful little bully."

"So if I come along next Saturday it will be alright?"

"Why don't you bring your dragon in tomorrow afternoon and we'll put her through her paces, shall we? It is better if you can get them used to the Coliseum before there's a big noisy crowd in there."

"Could I?" Eric grinned. "That would be great! I was a little worried about how she'd react to a crowd; I'm the only human she's ever had contact with—until this morning that is."

"Come here first and we'll fly in together, shall we?"

# 14

Eric lurched from a dream of the Gaol cell and the turnkey telling him to get some sleep before the tournament. He shook his head and abandoned a yawn as pain stabbed his cut cheek. He sat up and looked around, Tenebrozi and Azuria weren't on the ledge. He leapt to his feet and saw them down beside the stream, sitting on their haunches, side by side like jackrabbits they peered at something beyond the cave entrance.

"What are you two looking at?" Eric climbed down to join them. Tenebrozi puffed out a thin stream of smoke and Azuria swished the end of her tail. He crept to the entrance and immediately saw what had drawn the dragons' curiosity; a cloaked person sat on the rocks beside the stream gazing out to sea. Eric stayed in the shadows; he raised his hands to his mouth and mimicked the call of a bird that he'd often heard in the sand dunes. The person rose and searched for the source of the sound.

"Cateline!" Eric ran from the cave and scrambled down the rocks. "What are you doing here?" He halted a few paces from her. "What's happened?"

She had a livid mark on her cheek and a bruise on her neck; her eyes red and puffy.

"Eric!" She flung her arms around him, "I'm so glad I found you!"

As Eric led her into his cave, he noticed she limped. "What has happened? Who did this? Tell me, I'll kill them!"

"Onfroi has searched the nobility for a suitable match for his son, Aldus. He must have given up and decided I would suffice. Aldus didn't want to wait for a wedding. I packed my things and was about to leave when he came looking for me." She began to sob. "I had to fight him off, it's lucky he was very drunk. I kicked him where it hurts and while he was rolling about on the floor I grabbed my things and left. I stole Onfroi's cloak and ran as fast as I could. I can't go back, Eric! I don't want to marry that madman. I'll have to find another job!"

"You won't have to. I've got money, I can look after you." He helped her up to the ledge and sat her down on one of the wooden crates that served as his furniture. "Just sit there, you're safe now. I'll make some breakfast."

He stoked the fire and looked around for the dragons. They peeked over the ledge, wary eyes fixed on Cateline.

"Oh, come on you two!" It never occurred to him that dragons might be shy. Cateline shrunk back at the sight of the enormous creatures as they crawled up on to the ledge. "They're really quite harmless." Eric hoped they would not prove him wrong. He tethered them out of reach of his sister; he gave them their breakfast of dragon pellets. Tenebrozi blew out a thin stream of smoke.

At her inquiry, Eric explained to Cateline why he had a cut on his cheek.

She examined his damaged face. "We make quite a pair don't we?"

"But we'll survive, just as we've done since we were kids." Eric smiled and grimaced as the facial movement tugged on his wounded cheek.

He set about making breakfast of scrambled eggs and fried bread. He made tea and laid the largest of the crates with his mismatched cutlery and his only plate.

"It's nothing special but this place is my home. It's safe and dry, what more could I want?" He grinned and hoped to return some happiness to her face.

As she ate, Cateline relaxed. "You're quite a cook, little brother." She looked around at the messy ledge. "You could use a housekeeper though."

"Housekeeper!" Eric's mouth was a little too full. He swallowed hard, he'd just remembered Larkin's plight. "I know someone who needs a housekeeper!" He rubbed his chest—the hastily swallowed food jammed sideways. "Only if you want to—"

"That would be wonderful, but can I meet them first and decide?" Cateline perked up a bit after hearing this and agreed to come with Eric to meet Larkin that afternoon. "I'll have to keep my head down going into town, where is this place?"

"It's on the other side of the city and I wasn't planning to walk." Eric looked around at Azuria.

"Oh no!" Cateline read his mind. "I've never ridden a dragon and I don't intend to!"

"Azuria's very gentle!"

# 15

When Eric pulled Cateline up behind him on Azuria's back; the dragon looked around in surprise at having an extra passenger but didn't object. "Just put your arms around my middle and relax—and hold on."

Cateline's voice pitched up. "Oh! This is so high!"

Cold air stung their cheeks and eyes, the ships in King's Port Harbour tiny white smudges in the sapphire water, splashes of reflected sunlight dazzled their eyes. Castle Greycliff dominated the city foreshore; the serpentine mote circled and mauled the ramparts. Eric laboured to breathe with his sister's arms clamped around his torso. At his command, Azuria circled and landed on Larkin's gravel path. As Eric helped his sister down, an elderly man emerged from the house, his deep green robes flapped in the breeze.

"Hello there, can I help you?" Tall and thin, his white hair fluffed from under his fez.

"My name's Eric and this is my sister, Cateline. I was here last night. Is Larkin home?"

"Yes, come inside. I'm Milo, Larkin's gardener." He beckoned them to follow; along the hall, he pointed to a doorway. "He's there, in the kitchen. I'll go and fetch some salve for those cuts and bruises, you two look like you've been fighting."

"Eric!" Larkin lounged with one foot on the table and a cup resting in his lap. His eyes flew from Eric to Cateline, he sprang to his feet and the cup tinkled on the slate floor. His mouth moved but no words came out.

"Are you still looking for a housekeeper?"

"Ah—Um, yes!" Larkin's attention refused to leave Cateline.

Eric resisted the urge to laugh. He'd seen the great Dragon Ace, Larkin, full of confidence, swaggering around the Coliseum, beaming his charm to the ladies. This Larkin was a clumsy tongue-tied fool, goggling at Cateline. Eric tried to see his sister, not with the eyes of her brother but those of a man. She wore her dark hair pulled back and it fell in shining curls around her slender shoulders. In spite of the bruise, her face carried find-boned perfection, with clear blue eyes, ivory skin and full pink lips. His sister had grown into an exquisitely beautiful woman.

"Larkin," He broke the silence. "This is my sister, Cateline. She is in need of a job."

"Cateline!" A piece of china cracked under his foot as Larkin stumbled forward, took her hand and bowed. "Yes I need someone to do my house-cooking and keeping."

Cateline smiled, her dimpled cheeks turned pink. "I'm pleased to meet you, Mr Larkin"

It incensed Larkin and Milo when Cateline explained how she came by the bruises.

"Aldus is going to get what's coming to him one day. You're not the first woman he has used his fists on." He reached out to touch Cateline's face. "You'll be safe here, yes? If you have to go into the city either Milo or I will accompany you."

*************

After seeing Cateline settled into her new job, Eric accompanied Larkin to the Dragon Coliseum.

"I knew this place was big but standing here, it's—" Eric stopped, his voice bounced back at him.

"Do not worry about the echoes; they stop when the stands are full of people."

They stood with Azuria and Telzoth in the middle of the Coliseum. Azuria initially feared Telzoth, but after the flight from Larkin's house, she relaxed. Eric gazed at the stands, rising from the innermost seats to one-hundred and twenty feet at the back.

"So where do I begin?"

"We'll try the hoops first, shall we? I am guessing you'll know what's involved in that from having watched, no?"

"Yeah." Eric gazed at the hoops high above. "But watching is different to doing, I fear."

"We start from that end, yes?" Larkin pointed to the western end of the Coliseum. "Counting from one, you fly through twenty hoops without missing any, and you must go through in the right order—the numbers are written on them. You should do it in under a minute, every five seconds over loses you twenty points. Every five seconds under you're awarded an extra twenty points. Telzoth's personal best is forty seconds. The minute clock up there is wound around twice and it counts down two minutes. The horn sounds at one minute and again at two. After that—well, you're out of the running anyway."

Eric nodded and silently thanked Wischard for teaching him numbers.

Larkin continued, "So essentially, if your dragon goes through in just under a minute without hitting any of the hoops you're awarded two-hundred points. Every time a wing—or a whole dragon for that matter—hits a hoop, you lose twenty points."

"What if it's only a light touch?"

"Whenever anything hits the hoops hard enough to ring the Collision Bell in the judge's box up there, he hits the gong, yes?" He pointed to a stall at the top of the stands on the northern side. "The Collision Bell rings easily so you won't get away with much. I will go and lower the hoops, shall I? Wait here." He climbed on Telzoth and flew up to the judge's box. Eric watched as the hoops slowly sank to about sixty feet aloft. The green dragon returned and Larkin jumped off.

"Now." Larkin grinned. "This is where the superficial gobbledygook is called for, yes? Do not just start up there." He waved a hand towards the starting line. "You need to do a quick lap of the Coliseum before you start, no? You don't have to but the spectators love it, especially the ladies."

Eric had seen Larkin's gratuitous loops of the Coliseum, to grin and wave—whip the audience into a frenzy.

"I'm not sure if I'll be very good at posing, I think I'd feel like a dill."

"I did too when I was a lad like you, but when I learned the aces who bring the crowds get paid appearance money, my shyness vanished."

"Appearance money? Really? Just for appearing?"

"Yes. It is not well known—in fact it's not spoken of, but when I collect my prize money, I am always paid my bonus. I know of only one other rider who receives it but I am sure there are others."

Azuria only hit the rings a few times but took too long to complete the circuit; with Eric's urging, she improved but would still be out of contention.

"She's too timid—or maybe she just doesn't understand that she has to compete."

"Well she's not full grown yet." Larkin patted Azuria's neck. "She is a beautiful dragon. I think a good-looking fellow like you on a pretty, blue dragon will have you earning appearance money straight up. What's your other dragon like?"

"He's bigger and jet black. He's faster too, but harder to ride than Azuria."

"So let us go get him then, shall we?"

# 16

Larkin circled Tenebrozi, awestruck.

"Look at that bone structure! You say he is only a baby. We can expect great things from this beast, can we not?" He walked around, patting and admiring. Tenebrozi fidgeted at first, then a thin stream of smoke issued from his mouth; Eric relaxed, he took it as a sign the dragon had accepted Larkin. "Seems good natured too, many young dragons do not readily take to strangers."

Back at the Coliseum, Eric put Tenebrozi through the hoop course; the first time he completely missed three of them and knocked most of the rest with his wings. A few turns around the Coliseum, he improved and completed the course at a good pace, but two hours later, the Collision Bells still rang.

He settled in the centre of the Coliseum where Larkin waited with Telzoth and Azuria.

"He doesn't seem to get it at all," Eric complained.

Larkin looked puzzled. "Hmm."

*'You have to make him listen to you.'*

Eric looked around startled by a feminine voice. "Did—did you say something?" He frowned.

"No. Well nothing constructive." Larkin grinned.

"Did you hear that other voice?"

"No. There was no other voice."

*'Larkin cannot hear me, Eric.'* The voice spoke again. *'He is not Raigon-talth. He is not Venin Born.'*

Eric looked around puzzled, other than the three dragons, there was only Larkin.

*'It is me, Azuria. I am talking to you.'*

"Azuria?"

*'You don't have to speak aloud. I can hear your thoughts.'*

*'You can—'*

*'Hear your thoughts—yes. You are Raigon-talth, Eric. Venin Born, you have dragon blood; scratched by a Parinith hatchling. You are one of only three.'*

*'One of three? Where are the other two?'*

*'They will come for you in due course; you mustn't concern yourself with that. There is plenty of time. For now, you have to make Tenebrozi listen to you. It may be difficult.'*

*'How come? I can talk to you without even trying.'*

*'I am a healer and I'm female. We are better at communicating. Tenebrozi is a warrior; their minds are usually closed—as they must be, for their own protection.'*

*'You're a healer?'*

*'Yes. This is why I'm not good at flying through hoops.'*

*'I'm sorry—'*

Azuria's soft laughter resonated in his mind. *'I didn't mind, my sweet Eric. Go to Tenebrozi and try to connect.'*

"Eric? Did you hear what I said?" Larkin looked a little puzzled.

"Oh, sorry, I was thinking. What did you say?"

"I said, perhaps I'll fly Telzoth around the course and you follow on Tenebrozi. When he sees an experienced dragon take the course, he might catch on, yes?

"Yes, alright. But can I just lead him around on the ground for a few minutes first? It might calm him down."

"Sure." Larkin sank to the ground and leaned against Telzoth's leg.

Eric led Tenebrozi across the Coliseum, his face against his cheek.

'Tenebrozi' he spoke in his mind. 'Tenebrozi. Listen to me, Tenebrozi. Can you hear me?'

Nothing; Tenebrozi puffed out a long stream of smoke, he enjoyed this stroll across the Coliseum. Eric concentrated hard.

'Tenebrozi! Listen to me. Tenebrozi!' Tenebrozi propped and tilted his head. 'Can you hear me? Listen to me Tenebrozi!' Eric reeled as emotion stabbed, somewhere between joy and fear, a brief twinge of pain in his head and his heart leapt. 'Was that you Tenebrozi?'

Again, the emotional surge, the pain and his heart pulsed but this time Tenebrozi reared, a long blast of flames roared from his mouth.

'Whoa! Tenebrozi, it's me! Eric! Please don't be frightened!'

'Eric! Eric? That is your name—'

'Yes Tenebrozi, my name is Eric.'

'Why are you in my mind?'

'I want to talk to you. I promise I won't hurt you.'

'Eric. My Eric will not hurt me. No.' Intermittent puffs of smoke squirted from Tenebrozi's mouth.

'Of course I won't.'

'Eric?'

'Yes?'

*'Is there a reason why we have to fly through those round things above us? Wouldn't it be easier to go around them?'*

Eric laughed. How did one begin to explain silly human games to a dragon?

**************

Tenebrozi understood, through the hoops, without touching the hoops. Through the hoops, faster than any dragon has gone. *'Through the hoops! Eric wants me to fly through the hoops! Tenebrozi the Swift! That's my name!'* He enjoyed this game. *'Through the hoops! Faster and faster!'*

**************

Larkin whooped as Tenebrozi skidded to a halt beside him. "That must be a record!"

Eric jumped to the ground, laughing and hugged the scaly neck. Tenebrozi blew out a thin stream of smoke.

Larkin patted Tenebrozi's face. "That's amazing! How did you get him to do what you wanted, so quickly?"

"I talked to him. I told him what I wanted him to do."

"Talked—you talked to him?"

"Yes."

"Really?"

"In my mind. Azuria told me to do it."

"Azu—you talked to Azuria too? Th—the dragons talked back to you?"

"Yes."

75

"We better talk, yes? You and me." Larkin examined his face. "Yes," he muttered, "that would explain the hair—and the eyes." He studied the youth in front of him and nodded. "Come."

# 17

"Tell me again," said Milo, "exactly how you survived the scratch of a Parinith hatchling?"

Eric relived his life in words, from when the hatchlings emerged to today when he connected with Azuria and Tenebrozi.

"I know it sounds like I'm living in a fantasy world, but it's the truth."

Milo rose and stood before him. "No, Eric, it's not a fantasy. You are a Raigon-talth. There have been around fifty of them documented over the centuries. At this point in history there are only two, well three now you have shown up." Milo's cool fingertips raised Eric's face to his. "Remarkable. Your hair, eye colour, and your height are those of a Raigon-talth. You're much stronger and quicker than you were?"

"Yes, but I don't know if I'm stronger or quicker than any other boy my age."

"By the looks of you, I'd say you are stronger and quicker than a grown man." Larkin inhaled and pushed his chair back from the table and turned to Milo. "Well! Where to from here?"

"We should talk to Raulin."

"Who's Raulin?" Eric's gaze moved from Larkin to Milo. "And why do we have to talk to him?"

"Raulin is King Raulin." Milo smiled.

"You guys know the King?" Eric had information for the King.

Larkin nodded. Milo hastened away along the hallway. He returned a few minutes later.

"He'll see us now."

Larkin rose. "Let's go."

"What—now?" Eric smoothed his hair down and looked at his hands, at his tunic.

"It is fine, Eric," said Larkin, "Raulin is a kind-hearted man. Milo and I visited him once when we were covered in dragon dung."

"You were." Milo's brow puckered. "Dragon dung doesn't stick to me."

"We will put that to the test, no?"

"Come, we mustn't keep him waiting."

Eric followed Milo and Larkin along the hallway, down a flight of stairs and through a wooden door. In a darkened cellar, Milo reached between some shelves that held bottles of wine and wriggled something unseen. Beside the shelves, a hidden stone door squeaked and scraped open.

"Follow me." Milo took an oil lamp and hurried along a dark passage.

They descended four more flights of stairs, deeper and deeper the passage wound. On and on they walked. Eric opened his mouth to ask how much further when they began ascending; he counted five sets of stairs to a wooden door. Milo lifted the latch; it opened into a cellar. Another set of stairs later and they entered a brightly lit room. Outside, the fading daylight lit the ornate stained glassed windows.

"Welcome, Gentlemen!" A cheerful voice greeted them. A man sprang to his feet, violet robes rustled as he approached. His long white hair, flowing beard and moustache, contrasted with the dark brown eyes that pierced them from under shaggy brows. A black fez identical to Milo's perched on his head.

"Good evening, Reeve Calder!"

"Come, gentlemen! The King awaits."

Eric had never seen the King, even from a distance. He wiped the sweat from his palms as Calder led them along a short passageway, through an arched doorway and into a large, black and white marble-flagged room with more stained glass windows. Open with no seating, rows of marble pillars reared along each side. At one end, a raised dais boasted a timeworn throne of wood, leather, and brass. The candelabras stood unlit. Calder continued past the dais and opened the door beyond, into a smaller chamber.

"You're just in time gentlemen." A tall, young man rose from a chair by the fire. "I've instructed Ferrick to serve us supper in here." He stepped forward and shook hands with Milo and Larkin. "And this is the man-dragon." The King had a thin face with a neatly trimmed beard and moustache, he moved with straight-backed grace.

"This is Eric the Raigon-talth." Milo drew Eric forward. "Eric, meet King Raulin."

Eric bowed. "It's an honour to meet you, your Majesty."

"And it's an honour to meet you, Eric; your coming was long ago prophesized." The King smiled. "Welcome to Castle Greycliff. I'm sure you'll find it a most pleasant place to live."

"Live?" Eric straightened.

"Given that you are the long-awaited, third Raigon-talth, you'll have to be kept close, where we can keep an eye on you. The other two would not be impressed if I allowed you to wander off and get lost."

**************

An hour later, seated at the table Eric had the ear of the King, his personal aid, his cook, and two closest friends.

"Onfroi you say?" Reeve Calder puffed his pipe; smoke billowed toward the ceiling.

"You realise, young Eric that I should have you arrested?" The King frowned. Eric blenched, licked his lips and swallowed. This man had power a street kid could not imagine. "I outlawed Parinith dragons ten years ago." King Raulin smiled at Eric's anxious face. "But I won't. For one, it seems your rule breaking has given us our prophesized, third Raigon-talth. And if the theft of an illegal egg has helped a homeless orphan and his sister move up in the world then, in this instance, I will give a complete pardon."

Calder removed his pipe from his mouth. "What about Onfroi? You're not going to pardon his pilfering and plotting are you?"

"Indeed!" Ferrick scowled. "Onfroi deserves no pardon."

The King sighed. "My brother was supposed to be keeping an eye on his good friend. It would seem he's been neglecting his duty."

Eric swore he saw Calder, Ferrick, Larkin, and Milo squirm in their seats.

Calder leaned in. "Raulin, we could send someone else to surveil Onfroi's company."

"Let me talk to Randolf first. Yes, I know, Calder, he ran out of second chances years ago. But he's my brother—I have to trust him."

Eric saw Calder and Milo's eyes meet, their faces mirrored disquiet; Larkin frowned at the plate before him, and Ferrick gulped his wine.

**************

At Larkin's invitation, Eric settled Tenebrozi and Azuria into the vast dragon hall on Mistmere. He took a quick trip back to his cave, pocketed some of his stashed money and reburied the remainder. His meagre belongings fitted easily into the wooden crate he used as a table, and when he hid it behind a boulder, the cave appeared uninhabited.

# 18

The next morning, Reeve Calder introduced Eric to Prince Randolf, the King's younger brother, who would show him to the Elite Guard's tower. Shorter and stockier, Randolf bore little resemblance to his brother.

"You have been assigned to the King's personal guard," Randolf's eyes moved over Eric, taking in every detail. "Though I'm at a loss to explain how you have been given such a high post on your first day. Most new recruits have to work for years before they join the King's Elite. I believe you'll be the youngest ever appointed. You're awfully tall for a fifteen-year-old."

*Does he know what I am?*

Calder and Milo had instructed Eric to keep his Venin blood secret.

"I'll hand you over to Gilda shortly, but I'll first show you around. Won't hurt for you to know where everything is."

"Who's Gilda?"

"Gilda is the head of the King's Elite Guard, the Order of Galiron. Your training begins this afternoon."

Eric strolled the castle and grounds with Randolf, listening as the prince told him the history of his family, of King's Port and the wider Kingdom of Oldegoth.

"King Raulin was crowned ten years ago, at the age of sixteen, when our father, King Eustace the fourth, died suddenly. The physicians said he died from an unknown cause, but I think he was poisoned.

"I won't pretend that I approve how my brother rules this Kingdom. He hasn't increased taxes in five years; at this rate the crown will soon be bankrupt. He allows the people liberties I would never tolerate; they come and go without question. For all we know, there could be enemies coming here to destroy the Kingdom."

Eric said nothing, he didn't know what taxes were, nor did he know what bankrupt was. He knew of no enemies trying to enter the Kingdom but he did know one the Kingdom's worst enemies lived right there in King's Port.

Castle Greycliff was a small city inside ancient protective walls, its cobbled streets wound past the workshops. Eric's head turned this way and that as they passed the blacksmith where the steady rhythm of hammers pounded and shaped metal. The slush of heat against water startled him; vapour hissed and billowed from the open shopfront. Horses in the nearby stable nickered as the grooms poured oats into their troughs.

Eric coughed at strange odours from the armourer. "What is that smell?"

"Saltpeter and sulphur."

"What's that?"

"It's what our navy uses to fire their cannons. Although the way my pacifist brother runs the Kingdom, they're never likely to be fired again."

The clank of swords and challenges called out in practice gave way to wide flagstone paths winding to the spires that housed the Elite Guards, the Keep and the

King's tower far above. At the top of each spire grey and black flags flapped in the wind.

As they passed servants going about their daily tasks it disturbed Eric that most averted their eyes, gave a hasty bow or curtsy and hurried away. In the greenhouse, he saw a bent old man dressed in ancient leather sandals and a garment of rough spun cotton overlaid with a cloak made from a grain sack. On his head sprawled a filthy, squashed hat. Hunchbacked and dirty, he scrabbled along with one hand on the ground, a hickory staff clutched against his shoulder. He shuffled back into the shadow of a tall plant and glared at Randolf.

"Hello, Nutley." Randolf lifted his chin." I hope you're behaving yourself."

Nutley exhaled a soft, wheezing hiss. The plant beside him squirted a jet of green liquid. Randolf skittered sideways; the liquid fell to the ground and fizzled. A wispy cloud of white smoke wafted an eye-watering stench into the air.

They reached the door and Eric looked back; the old man hobbled onto the path to glare after him. As Eric turned away, the man pressed his finger to the side of his nose and cleared his nostril into a plant pot.

"What—who was that?" Eric shivered.

"That's Nutley; he's crazy as a loon. He's worked for my family around ten years. He does nothing but sneak around, scaring people and growing dangerous plants. Steer clear of him—he hates everyone." Randolf glanced up at Eric as they ascended ancient stone stairs leading back to the keep. "My brother insists he stay in the confines of the castle, says he'll be treated badly if turned on the street. Personally, I think he should be locked up;

he's a menace. He's a slippery little worm too, every time I try to catch him he vanishes. Don't be fooled, he's a lot agiler than he looks."

"Hail Randolf!" A voice came from their left. A tall, solidly built man approached from the upper bailey, he wore the garb of a knight—black leggings and tunic with silver buckles and boiled leather armour.

"Sir Cesper!" Randolf saluted, "are you well?"

"I'm always well." Sir Cesper's amber-eyed gaze settled on Eric.

"Sir Cesper, this is the latest recruit to the King's Elite Guard, his name is Eric."

"Welcome to Castle Greycliff, Eric, and to the service of our King." Cesper grinned.

"Thank you, Sir Cesper," Eric bowed, unsure how to greet a knight of the realm.

"We'll catch up for an ale sometime. Well, I must press on, I'm on duty."

Eric looked back as they continued up the stairs; Cesper continued toward the Gatehouse, exchanging pleasantries with everyone he passed.

"I never knew there were so many people inside the fortress. Where do all these people live?"

"Most of the lower workers live outside in the city. The gate and perimeter guards live down there, beside the Gate Tower." Randolf twisted and pointed back to a building beside the gate. "The Elite Guard live in that tower there. The younger knights live in that other tower—the older knights live in the city. The pages and squires stay wherever their knight-master requires them to be."

"What do the knights do?"

"Here in Oldegoth they can be many things—guards, spies. Sometimes they accompany the King or others of the nobility on diplomatic missions. When there is a war on, they lead the peasant army into battle. But come— let's eat. Then I'll take you to Gilda."

# 19

After lunch, Randolf escorted him up the winding path to the Elite Guard's tower.

"Just go in." Randolf nodded." They're expecting you. I won't stop, I have work to do this afternoon so I'll wish you luck and leave you here." He shook Eric's hand; his smile didn't reach his eyes.

"Thanks for showing me around."

**************

Eric entered the double doors and looked around. The place appeared deserted. Ahead, a door opened on a haphazard array of clay pots of flowers and herbs. The sunlight through the arched windows dazzled Eric's eyes. A voice spoke from somewhere among the plants.

"So Randolf has finished his scrutiny?" A grey-haired woman stepped into view, scissors in one hand and a bunch of flowers in the other. She wore black leggings and a grey tunic. Her brown eyes sparkled as she approached. She tucked the scissors into her pocket and held out her hand, "I'm Gilda. You'll be Eric, the Raigon-talth." She dropped the last word to a whisper. She had a small crown symbol inside a circle tattooed on her forehead.

"Oh! You're Gilda? Um, yes—I'm Eric."

She smiled. "You weren't expecting a woman. Most people don't expect the head of the King's Elite to be a woman." Gilda turned and called through a door to her right, "Tomas!"

"Yes Gilda, he's gone." The voice came from the opposite direction. A man dressed the same as Gilda moved catlike through the door behind. "And this'll be our new recruit!"

Tomas was nearly as tall as Eric but double his weight. He had a deep voice and a cheerful face. Bald with a silver hoop through one earlobe and on his forehead the same tattoo as Gilda. He shook Eric's hand.

"Well, let's get the lad outfitted and we'll begin training." Gilda moved to a nearby table, stuffed the flowers into a mortar and began crushing them with a pestle. "Show him to his quarters too, please Tomas."

**************

Eric spent weeks training with fists, sticks, and swords; he learned to use a bow. He improved and received fewer bruises with each passing week. He trained with Tomas mainly, but torturous sessions with a girl called Clarice taught him to fight with a wooden quarterstaff. She refreshed his bruises and stirred a new emotion. He'd never had close physical contact with any girl other than his sister. The blue depths of her eyes reflected the sun, clouds, and sky.

"Ow!" Eric hit the ground hard. Clarice held him with her quarterstaff. She scrambled to her feet and cleared her throat.

"Come on, try again." She resumed her stance. "No—you hold a quarterstaff like this—like that, you'll lose balance."

Musical clunks punctuated their shouts and laughter as they parried. Eric gained the upper hand and pinned her to the ground. He smiled, held her down and gazed into her eyes.

"This is fun."

"Eric," Clarice's chest heaved. "You should let me up now."

Her words seeped into his conscience, and as he pulled her to her feet, his dragon heart beat with vigour beyond physical exertion.

In the next session, he learned hand-to-hand combat with Haman, a wiry, pinched-faced man of forty; he kicked Eric around the bailey for hours before Eric could land a return kick.

He relished living and training with the Elite Guard. They opened his mind to the wider world as he sat in the mess hall of an evening and listened to his fellow guardsmen's conversations. All but Clarice—who hadn't completed her training—carried the encircled crown tattoo. There were twenty Elite Guard, though never more than five or six in the mess hall at a time. Guard duty spanned all hours of the day and night. They warned Eric to keep quiet in the sleeping quarters as members of the Elite slept in shifts around the clock.

One evening, seated at the table in the mess with Clarice, Gilda, and Haman, the conversation came around to the Raigon-talth and Eric admitted he knew little about them.

"I've never heard the prophecy." He shrugged at Haman's inquiry and his eyes returned to Clarice where they wanted to stay.

Clarice rose, rummaged through the trunk in the corner and took out a brass cylinder. She pulled a cork from one end and withdrew a rolled parchment. She stretched it out on the table, her eyes travelled down the script.

"Here it is." She cleared her throat and began reading. "'When the dead bell tolls, seven wizards of olde, restore the order of Saint Alúthien. Dragons, four score and hundreds more, and the Raigon-talth three, shall gather for war. Of the venin born throng, the'—and we can't read this part—'through the murk. Oldegoth must fight—and this is another bit we can't read—'once more.'"

She let the scroll spring closed. "It's a very old piece of parchment; some of the ink has faded so we cannot read all. But the first bit is clear."

"There is just one problem with that prophecy." Gilda tapped the table with a forefinger. "It says seven wizards and we only have six. There have only been six for some years. The other was Hectar; he was beaten to death in the street. They never caught those responsible. His body is in a tomb in the crypt under the King's tower."

"But there are seven wizards." Haman set his cup on the table. "There is Tagrali."

"Tagrali? Isn't he a myth?" Eric's scalp prickled as he remembered the scary stories his father told of Tagrali.

"Tagrali is no myth."

"But Haman, Tagrali was denounced and expelled from the order long ago."

"He's still a wizard."

"From everything I've read on the subject, he's a failed wizard—hence his epithet, 'Failed Wizard Tagrali.'"

"Wizards? There are wizards?" Eric gazed from face to face around the table. "Real magic men?"

"Calder is a wizard as well as being Reeve of King's Port," said Haman, "I don't know of any more, they don't show themselves much."

"There's Milo, Ferrick, and others," said Gilda.

"Milo? I thought he was just Larkin's gardener." Though now Eric thought about it, Milo didn't dress like a gardener.

"Yes, Milo. He's the head of The Order since Hectar died." Gilda stood, "but that's enough chatter for one night, off to bed all of you. Eric, you will begin guard duty tomorrow. You and Haman will be first shift guarding the crown in the morning and then tomorrow afternoon it'll be more training."

"The crown?" Eric frowned.

"The Galiron Crown, at the top of The Keep. The King's Elite Guard is also known as The Order of Galiron. The crown is most coveted artefact in the Kingdom. Seized from a tyrant long ago and entrusted to an ancient King of Oldegoth by Gyarie, the Goddess of Serasya."

"Serasya? Where's that?"

"Just sail twenty miles north of here through the Dorcliff Channel and you're in the Kingdom of Serasya. It's on the map, there on the wall." Clarice drew him to a parchment map and ran her finger across a landmass towards the top.

"Um, I can't read." Eric's ears burned; three years older, Clarice knew much more than he did. Her eyes moved from the map to search Eric's face, he could see the candlelight and himself reflected in her eyes as she gazed up at him.

Gilda's voice broke the tension. "After your training session tomorrow come to the flower room. I'll begin teaching you." She moved to the door. "We can't have a Raigon-talth who is illiterate."

Clarice smiled. "Goodnight, Eric."

# 20

During an afternoon off, Eric strolled around the fortress. As he passed the blacksmith, a familiar voice hailed.

"Eric?"

Eric turned and his friend Yrian stood in the door with a hammer in his hand.

"Yrian, I didn't know you worked in here."

"I didn't know you did either. I haven't seen you for ages—I almost didn't recognise you."

"Why?"

"You've changed."

"Um, yeah—so I have. How long have you worked here?"

"I started last week—still pinching myself—I'm working for the King! I thought I saw him yesterday but my boss said it wasn't him. What are you doing here?"

"Training for the—oh just training to be a guard." Eric had already learned to keep his mouth closed about the Elite Guard—most greeted his new position with disbelief.

"Well, I better get back to work." Yrian looked at his steely-eyed boss.

"Me too. Let's catch up sometime and have a drink."

**************

Gilda presented Eric's lessons on thin slabs of slate in a wooden frame. He wrote his answers with a thin stick of talc rock. Eric finished writing his sentences and laid the slate on Gilda's workbench. He had made good progress with his reading and writing.

Gilda looked up from the plant she worked on. "Before you go for your training session, can you take that hairy sedge-lily and that thorn apple plant to the greenhouse? Tell Nutley my experiment was a failure and tell him, thanks for the advice and for the loan."

"Um—okay."

"You got that?"

"Yes—I—your experiment failed, thanks for the advice and for the loan."

"Very good."

Eric grinned, tucked a pot into the crook of each arm, and headed for the greenhouses. The place seemed deserted as he searched for somewhere to place the plants.

"The gangly man-dragon has come alone this time—I wonder why?"

The plants slipped in Eric's arms as he spun to see who spoke. Nutley glowered at him from the shadow of a plant that swayed without the aid of a breeze.

"Oh, good morning, Nutley!"

"Mornings are never good, Eric Man-Dragon." Nutley gave a wet sniff.

"Man-Dragon?"

A large purple plant, tied with thick rope inside an iron cage caught Eric's attention. As he watched, it extended a coiling tendril towards Nutley. The old man snipped off the tendril, dropped it to the ground and held it there with his hickory staff.

The pale eyes narrowed. "I hope my plants are undamaged."

Eric shrugged, "They look pretty good."

Nutley hissed.

"Ah—now let me think—Gilda said—"

"Her experiment failed and thanks for the advice—not that she listened—she never listens." Nutley pressed a finger to his nose and blew a glob of mucus into a nearby barrel of horse dung.

Eric set the plants on a bench. "Yes, that and thanks for the loan."

"The King never listens either."

"Um—"

Nutley's lips framed a remembered conversation and his eyes narrowed. "Should have knocked that one on the head when he was a pup," he mumbled.

"Huh—who?"

Nutley wheezed and shuffled past to examine his plants, he seemed to have forgotten he had company. While the old man muttered and wheezed to himself, Eric retreated.

**************

For the first time in their fifteen years of life, Eric and Yrian entered the Fishermen's Inn, the waterfront tavern, accompanied by Sir Cesper. Warm and noisy, the dimly lit tavern hosted people from all walks—from whores and sailors to merchants and aristocrats. The cold wind rushed in with each new arrival though none complained; the stifling atmosphere benefited from frequent ventilation. In the corner, a group of musicians clanked, scraped, and squeaked; a woman warbled in sweet defiance of the discordant accompaniment. A white-haired Serasyan sailor waltzed with a lady of the night while the band played a jig.

"Come, lads," Cesper raised his voiced over the hubbub. "Let me buy you both a pot of ale."

The boys seated themselves at a table near the window as Cesper wove his way to the bar. He returned to thump three ale pots on the table and slid one each to Eric and Yrian. The light through the window faded as the boys acquainted themselves with Sir Cesper, King Raulin's chief knight; the finest in the kingdom. His amber eyes danced merrily as he stretched out his long legs, sipped ale and entertained them with amusing anecdotes.

"How did you come to be a knight?" Eric grinned as Yrian took a mouthful of ale and shuddered.

"I got a job with the gate guards when I was twelve, one day I was messing around with some of the lads, jousting with sticks and one of the knights saw me. He must have thought I was all right; he invited me to become a squire. That was eight years ago—now I'm a Knight of the Realm of Oldegoth."

"More important than making horseshoes in the smithies." Yrian took another slurp of his ale.

"It might seem like dull work but without a good blacksmith the castle wouldn't function." Cesper poured a draft of ale down his throat.

"It seems my main task is to guard the Galiron Crown."

"And a very important job it is too. There are some who would like to steal it."

"What would they use it for?"

Don't know but it would make a handsome doorstop."

Eric laughed and wondered if Cesper knew more than he let on. There seemed an element of mystery surrounding the Galiron Crown.

"Were you born here? In King's Port?"

"Yes, I grew up in the orphanage." Cesper set his drink on the table and straightened. "Well, well, well, if it isn't the lovely Clarice."

Eric inhaled a little of his ale as his head swivelled to the door; Clarice, Haman, Nalfar, and Derrin huddled together and cast about for a table.

Cesper waved to them. "Elite Guards! Come and join us!"

Eric coughed and brushed his top lip, fearing he might share Yrian's ale-froth moustache.

As the evening wore on, the crowd and noise increased, Eric's heart raced as he danced with Clarice. He moved in closer but she smiled and returned him to arm's distance. The Serasyan sailor joined the musicians to sing a raucous drinking song, punctuated with belches, and pauses to gulp ale. Eric stared as a group of tall, slant-eye people entered. Their long, straight hair stood in spikes and fell past their shoulders; their pointed ears poked through their hair.

"Who are those strange looking people?"

Clarice turned to follow his gaze and flinched; she spun Eric around. "They're Slokks from Belcliff Island. Don't look at them. They'll challenge you to a fight if you make eye contact. You won't win."

**************

97

After midnight, the group roamed along Castlebridge Road back to Castle Greycliff, chatting and laughing. Eric thought himself the only one to notice Sir Cesper peel off to speak to a tall, cloaked figure in the shadows. By the time they reached the drawbridge, Cesper had re-joined them.

"A friend of yours?" Eric whispered.

"One of my informants. There is more to being a knight than jousting."

The words, 'What's an informant?' hovered on the tip of Eric's tongue but he closed his mouth on them.

**************

Saturday morning and Eric had the day off. Today would be his first appearance at the coliseum and he wanted to invite Clarice to accompany him but feared he'd make a fool of himself while she watched.

*Let's see how good you are before you show off.*

He arrived at Larkin's house as the sunrise flared on the eastern horizon and promised fine weather.

"Eric, you're just in time for breakfast!" Larkin accompanied him to the kitchen.

"I don't know if I can eat anything this morning."

"What's the matter?" Cateline looked up as she set the table. "Are you sick? You're always hungry."

"Just nervous."

"You'll feel better if you eat something, yes?" Larkin pulled a chair out for Cateline and Eric smiled as the dragon ace fussed over his sister. "Come, Eric, sit and eat."

Eric took Larkin's advice and ate a bowl of porridge. The butterflies in his stomach stopped fluttering.

"Now, my beautiful Cateline, you are ready to watch the dragon tournament, no?"

"I look forward to it." Cateline smiled, her cheeks turned pink.

Eric pretended not to notice Larkin's soppy smile as he tweaked her nose. He imagined doing the same to Clarice and feared she might break his arm in response to such familiarity.

**************

Tenebrozi balked at the noisy crowd in the stands as they flew behind Telzoth; Eric watched Larkin wave and blow kisses—playing to the crowd. Eric hung on and tried to calm his dragon. From the centre of the Coliseum, an announcer shouted through a large horn, Eric caught snatches of his spiel.

"…the greatest ever dragon ace! Larkin on Telzoth the Magnificent!"

The crowd roared over his words.

"…new to the Dragon Coliseum, Eric on Tenebrozi the Swift! We shall see how swift he really is, shall we folks? Also, today we have…"

*'Why are there so many people today, Eric?'*

*'They've come to watch us—they want to see how well you can fly.'*

*'I fear my wings might fall off, Eric.'*

*'Nonsense! Just ignore the people and fly like you've done during practice.'*

"…followed by Lucretia the Fierce on Syrelz Razor Fang! And last but not at all the least, Balien the

99

Honourable on Razielia the Red. Balien is the proprietor of the King's Port Dragon Hatchery, President of the Dragon Breeders Guild, an ethical breeder of fine dragons and major sponsor of The Dragon Colesium!"

**************

The tournament over, Eric gathered with Cateline, Larkin, Balien, Lucretia, and the other Dragon Aces. Nerves aside, he estimated Tenebrozi's performance above average. Larkin thought so too.

"Well done, Eric and Tenebrozi! You have proven yourselves equal to all today, no? Your very first day and you placed in hoops!" Larkin scratched Tenebrozi's scaly head. "Excellent performance!"

"So, where did you steal that dragon from, boy?"

Eric looked around to see who spoke. Wilmot's mouth twisted in an evil grin as he emerged from the steward's office. Eric's hand shot out, grabbed the front of Wilmot's tunic and lifted him off the ground.

"Eric!" Cateline plucked at his sleeve. "You shouldn't—"

The dragon ace's around them hooted and cheered.

"Wring his neck, Eric!" Lucretia's face shone with ferocious anticipation. "Give him a long, blue tongue!"

"Shake him, Eric—"

"Drop him on his fat head!"

Larkin grinned at Wilmot's discomfit, slipped his arm around Cateline's shoulders and drew her away.

"Don't you have any work to do?" Eric hoisted Wilmot higher.

"Yes, unlike you, 'dragon ace.'"

100

"Then go and do it." Eric threw Wilmot into a pile of dragon dung.

"Eric," Balien brushed an imaginary speck off Razielia's gleaming face and the red queen nuzzled her owner's hand. "I'd like to speak to you sometime about using the services of your beautiful black dragon."

"Oh? Why? What for?"

"For breeding of course!"

"Oh, I see." Eric's ears burned.

"I'd love to mix the blood of your black with a fine, scarlet like Razielia. You see, it's my belief that breeding the common reds with the rarer species will…"

*'Isn't my Balien sweet, Eric Man-dragon?'* Razielia batted her pink eyelids and puffed a delicate cloud of white smoke.

# 21

The King's scout, Vildar, bowed and stood to attention, his eyes fixed on Raulin's.

Raulin regarded the weary man. He looked as though he had ridden hard and not slept for days.

"What did you find, Vildar?"

"Sire, I've sighted a large gathering just outside the province of Yellowill. In my estimate, about five-hundred men. There is a makeshift smithy on site, making a lot of noise, probably creating weapons. They have many horses and at least fifty dragons, Sire." The scout rubbed a weary hand over his face and swallowed.

Raulin snapped his fingers at a servant. "Give the man some wine."

"Thank you, your Majesty. I returned as fast as I could."

"You've done well. You weren't seen by anyone?"

"No, Sire."

"Very well, Vildar. Ferrick," Raulin called to his cook and valet, "serve Vildar a kingly breakfast."

"Sire, there's just one more thing you should know."

Raulin turned back to Vildar.

"Sire, Lord Onfroi was there with his son, Aldus; it appeared they held command. And I found this, blowing across the field at the edge of the woods where I hid." He pulled out a scrap of soiled parchment and passed it to the King.

"Onfroi is not a lord, Vildar," Raulin took the parchment and shook it straight. "He would like to be but I can be royally obstinate when the mood takes me. Like my father before me, I don't hand out peerages unless they're deserved." He frowned as he read the hand-printed script.

*'Food and warm clothing to all who join The New Order of Oldegoth, Saffron Field, Yellowill. Come and fight for us and you will have two meals a day and a purse of coins when victory is ours. Share in the new prosperity.'*

The King chuckled. "Trust Onfroi to assume everyone can read. Still, this is grave news indeed, I will need to think on this and consult my advisers. Thank you, Vildar. Now go and eat then get some rest. Take two days off duty."

**************

Guttering candles cast ghostly shadows on the walls of Castle Greycliff's war room.

"…we have the option to mount an all-out attack and arrest Onfroi but it has become evident that someone within these walls appears to be his accomplice. We might miss our chance to end this insurrection once and for all."

Raulin finished speaking, his eyes moved from face to face. Gilda, the wizards, Milo, Giles, Wischard, Ferrick, Hawser, and Calder sat along one side of the table, on the other, Sir Cesper with his highest knights, Sir Kilburn, Sir Albiron, and Sir Dowden. The same emotion etched on all their faces: weariness, anger, and a willingness to fight.

"What I have told you must not leave this room. Not until we discover what Onfroi's intentions are."

"How are we to do that?" asked Calder.

"We will have to send a spy into his midst. Shouldn't be too hard given he is accepting men with open arms."

"One of the Elite Guard?"

"Would that be an imposition, Gilda?"

"Gentlemen, you're forgetting something," said Gilda. She pointed to the tattoo on her forehead. "Clarice hasn't earned hers yet but regardless, we can hardly send a pretty girl into a platoon of men."

"Oh yes." Sir Cesper grinned.

"I'll give you all time to think about it," Raulin drained his cup and pushed back his chair. "Sleep on it and we'll talk again in the morning."

Cesper raised his finger. "We have one thing in our favour—Castle Grey Cliff has never been breached in the five hundred years since it was built."

Calder waited for the King to rise then got to his feet. "That's true. Unless someone opens the gate and invites the enemy in, we're safe. Of that you can be sure, but what of the people of the city? What of the people of Oldegoth?"

"We will need to call on our warriors." Cesper spoke over the scraping of chairs. "Perhaps we could recall those who patrol the Parinith Strait."

"Yes, Cesper. Send a messenger on a dragon. Order the Admiral to send all but one ship back to King's Port Harbour."


**************

Eric sat quietly, working through the sums Gilda had set for him, the thin pencil shrieked on the slate and gave him goose bumps. The early morning sun slanted into the flower room and the pots of yellow daisies distracted him as they bent, straining towards the light. Gilda entered the room as he finished the last calculation and passed her the slate.

Gilda's eyes flicked down the rows of numbers. "That's good. You're making great progress, Eric."

"Gilda, those plants are moving."

"Yes, they're xanthous heliotropic daisies, commonly called butter daisies."

"But why—"

"Plants need the sun to grow, Eric. Some plants actively seek it."

"Why do you have them?"

"Mainly because I like plants but I also keep them for their medicinal properties."

Eric opened and closed his mouth—many questions queued on his tongue.

"If you're interested in plants, someday I'll teach you about them. But not today—now that the first part of your training is finished, I have a mission for you—if you're up for it."

"Sure—what do you want me to do?"

"Well, it will require discretion..."

***************

Eric followed Gilda's order and presented himself at the blacksmith to have a battle-helm fitted.

"This is no ordinary battle-helm, Master Eric." Rolly the Blacksmith grinned. "Master Yrian was ordered to make this one."

"Good!"

"Normally I would say it's not good for he is a mere apprentice but in this case, we want the helm to look as if made by a peasant farmer."

"I—I see."

"You're wondering why, I think."

"Well—yes."

"I haven't the faintest notion why they want such a helm but who am I to argue when the order comes from the tower."

The helmet, a flat-topped creation, shadowed Eric's eyes.

It reverberated with Yrian's laughter. "I must say, that is the silliest thing I have ever seen."

"You made it." Eric's voice rang inside the miscreation.

"Now, Eric. I have been instructed to take you to Reeve Calder." Rolly removed his leather apron and hung it on the wall.

"Already? But I'm on duty."

"I believe this is part of your duty, Eric. My orders were to bring you to the tower."

"They're not wasting any time."

"I guess not."

**************

Eric tapped on the door and it sprung open.

"Eric, come in, lad." Calder and Milo poured over a map they had laid across a mess of parchment and scrolls on the table. Raulin gazed out the window, his hands linked behind his back.

Eric studied the door. *Did it just open all by itself?*

"We have a job for you, Eric—do you own some old shabby clothes?"

"None that fit me anymore."

"Never mind, we'll provide them. Now listen carefully…"

# 22

Eric slipped his whetstone back into his rucksack and touched a fingertip to the razor-sharp blade. The sword hissed back into its scabbard and he peered over the heads of his comrades to spy on the circle of tents from where he knew Onfroi would come. The men around him chatted and argued as they too, tended their weapons. The sun winked out and sank, a blanket of darkness crept over the land. Eric coughed as one of his companions fanned fire into a pile of sticks, billowing smoke gave way to flames.

"Who'd ya reckon Lord Onfroi is bringin' for an inspection?" Ramsey scanned the men around him with pink-piglet eyes and thumbed the blade of his axe. His pointed helmet with badly attached ram's horns allowed a froth of blond curls to hug his bull-neck.

"Dunno." A lank-haired youth lounged against an elm trunk and gnawed on a discoloured piece of jerky. Eric frowned at the sword stabbed into the mud. The flat-topped helmet he thought might have once served as a cooking pot. "Dun affect us none."

Eric could think of nothing that would affect them more. The person arriving to inspect them might be the most dangerous man in the Kingdom. It would take more than just Onfroi to organize an attack of this scale.

*How many of these recruits' families live in King's Port and have they considered what might become of them if they overthrow the King?*

Eric didn't comment, he had been instructed to keep a low profile—don't attract attention. Assess the situation and leave in the middle of the night. He'd arrived on foot; riding in on a dragon would have ruined his cover.

He recalled Calder's words. *"Report back to Castle Grey Cliff, then you will go to Dorcliff to join the Raigon-talth."*

While training with Onfroi's recruits, he kept his performance to average; anything above or below would draw the drill sergeant's scrutiny.

"Awright you lazy layabouts! On your feet for an inspection by the commander in chief! Stand, form a line and present arms!" The drill sergeant repeated his words as he passed each group. The men scrambled to their feet and formed a line along the path. Easily the tallest man in the company, Eric positioned himself beside Ramsey, hoping the sham of a helmet would distract attention from himself. His feet began to hurt as they waited. At last, the drill sergeant, Onfroi and his guest came into view. Eric stole a look at the approaching party and his stomach lurched; Prince Randolf, resplendent in full battle regalia strode towards him.

Eric's heart pounded in his ears; though he found it hard to stand still, he knew running would only call attention to himself. He prepared to identify himself as Wilkin son of Wain and vehemently deny his own name. He hoped his dirty face and the ugly helm sufficient disguise. His height, his eyes, and the scar on his cheek could betray him. He inhaled and mentally rehearsed the lies he, Milo and Calder had constructed about his assumed identity—the ready explanation that his father gave him the scar while teaching him respect. He took a calming breath and repeated the details of 'Wilkin, son of Wain.' Eric was confident his green eyes wouldn't glow in partial light; only in pitch dark would they give him away. Eric kept his head down, slouching and bending his knees a little, to make himself appear shorter. Onfroi and Randolf came to a halt close to Eric. They interrogated a couple of recruits opposite, turned, and proceeded without a glance in his direction. He exhaled and waited until they disappeared.

The Drill sergeant moved down the line. "Awright! Bed!"

Eric called from the shadow of the elm. "Can I relieve myself first, sir?"

"Go on. You men are like girls..." He muttered and turned away.

Eric shouldered his rucksack and hurried away into the dark. He removed the helmet, tossed it down a latrine as he passed by and raised the hood of his cloak. He passed horse enclosure to the tethered line of dragons and concentrated on the green dragon before him.

*'Isuthiel. Isuthiel—please talk to me. Isuthiel. It's me, Eric. You were my dragon.'*

*'I was your dragon but you sold me.'* The unexpected reply came with the rush of emotion—anger, hurt, a stab of pain, his heart convulsed.

*'I'm sorry, Isuthiel. I didn't want to sell you but I needed money. I'm very sorry. I hope you're now owned by someone who cares for you properly.'*

*'My master, Aldus, is going to have my claws removed.'*

*'What? Removed!'*

*'Yes, chopped off. Tomorrow it will happen. I'm going to be made defenceless.'*

*'Listen to me, Isuthiel. I'm not staying here. Tonight, I'm leaving. If you want, I'll come for you and we'll leave together. My orders are to report to the King and then join the Raigon-talth.'*

*'We can leave tonight?'*

*'Yes, tonight.'*

*'Yes. Yes tonight, we leave.'*

Eric knew Isuthiel hadn't yet forgiven him. A thread of hurt and anger interwove the words of their telepathic dialogue, but with these last words, he detected mounting hope.

*'You can stay with me, I won't sell you again. Or you can go to Dorcliff Island and become a wild dragon like you were born to be. My dear Isuthiel, you don't have to stay in the service of men. You are bigger and stronger than any man that walks this world, if you don't like them—if they hurt you, you can leave. You are a free dragon. All dragons are free.'* A rush of tears blurred Eric's vision, something deep in himself and Isuthiel wept, lamenting the loss of childhood. The loss of a parent's love. Missed years of youth, snatched away by fate and greed. The tears on Eric's face were those of the human child and the dragon child. Isuthiel and the dragons around them wept for the loss of home and family. Their grief tugged on Eric's heart.

*'None of you has to stay here'* He projected his mind to them all. *'You are all strong and intelligent beings, if you do not like it here, come with Isuthiel and me, we will leave tonight.'*

*'Yes! Yes! Tonight! We leave tonight!'*

*'The ropes that bind you are weak; if you can't break them, burn them! Be ready my brothers and sisters. We leave tonight.'*

*'I gave you, your Venin Blood. You are my brother.'* Then Isuthiel spoke to the dragons around him, *'I gave Eric his Venin Blood, he is of the Raigon-talth. I gave him the power to free us all.'*

*'Be ready to leave as soon as I return.'* Eric untied Isuthiel's tether. *'Be ready. All of you.'* He hugged the green dragon's neck.

Eric crept through the dark and stopped behind a row of tents. Onfroi and Randolf's voices issued through the canvas.

"…enough information to use against Larkin. Someone like that, being close to the King. It could be perceived as dangerous to the Kingdom. We can cast suspicion on him—make the people distrust him—you know—we could argue they wouldn't just send us a free hostage to keep until we were ready to use him."

"Well of course they wouldn't, but—"

"And, we can accuse the King of consorting with undesirables—foreign enemies—the Serasyans are not allies of Oldegoth."

"Neither are they enemies—"

"But our people don't know that—our people know little at all about The Invisible Kingdom—some of them doubt it even exists! Now we know who Larkin is we must use it to our advantage. The King must be deposed for his own good, placed under house arrest—if the people know why, they'll support us."

"Either way, we'll have enough men sufficiently trained to mount an attack," Onfroi's voice greased its way to Eric's ears. "I say we go with our original plan.

Attack in the middle of the night. It's simple, you on the inside will open the gate and allow our foot soldiers entry. We who have dragons can move in quickly, kill the King and have you installed as the new monarch before sunrise."

"I told you, it won't be that simple. The knights and guards on the gate keep it heavily fortified, day and night. If you are able to get past them, you then have to get to the King. There are about twenty elite guards, not many, I know! I know! But you haven't seen them in action, I have and I tell you now, you'll have difficulty getting past them. Give me another day or so to try and shore up our support on the inside." Silence filled the moment before Randolf spoke again. "I do not want my brother killed! I don't want that on my conscience. Just—just place him under arrest. That would be sufficient."

"Your brother murdered his King father."

"What if you're proven wrong, Onfroi?"

"He and Hectar the wizard. Kingslayers, both of them. I tell you, they killed him. Poisoned him with arsenic."

Eric's heart quickened—did Raulin murder his father?

"How can I be sure? How do I know it wasn't someone else poisoning him?"

"We've been through this before—"

"How do I know, the stuff you gave me to sprinkle on his food wasn't the toxin which killed him?"

"It was an antidote to Raulin's poison. The King was my good, dear friend! Why would I want to kill him?"

Beads of sweat damped Eric's face. *'Onfroi wants to kill Raulin!'*

A sound from his left startled him.

Someone shouted in the dark. "Who goes there?"

A guard had detected Eric's presence. Eric ran, his long Raigon-talth strides easily outpaced those in pursuit. His emerald green eyes guided him through the dark. He leapt onto Isuthiel's back and the green dragon spread his wings, with a few beats he soared over the trees and away, the other dragons followed. Eric hung on as Isuthiel accelerated into the night.

*'Home! We're going home!'* The joyous thoughts of the dragons came to Eric through the black night air. *'To our motherland! Away we fly! Home!'*

The roar of wind in his ears drowned the shouts of Onfroi's men and the horses' whinnies. Around him, the dragons screeched gleefully as they sped away to freedom; happiness lent them vigour.

High in the sky, Eric fretted and replayed Randolf and Onfroi's conversation in his mind—anger and fear seared his gut. What was it about Larkin? Was he from Serasya? Eric guessed he wasn't originally from Oldegoth, the accent, the pale hair, and golden skin gave that away. Eric had seen men disembarking ships in King's Port Harbour that looked and spoke like Larkin. He wished he'd heard more, was his friend of dubious character? Cateline lived in his house; she worked for him. Eric's every instinct told him Larkin was a man of honour. What if his instinct proved wrong? In an effort to remove her from peril, had he sent his sister into worse danger?

*'They're calling for you, my Eric. The Venin Born are calling—can you hear them?'* Isuthiel's thoughts broke into his worried contemplation.

*'I will go to them later tonight.'*

*'We go now.'* Isuthiel veered north and crossed the coastline.

*'I'm supposed to report to the King!'*

*'The Venin Born command your presence, Eric. I must bring you to them.'*

**************

"What do you mean it was a man-dragon?" Onfroi snapped. "There's no such creature as a man-dragon!"

"I tell you, Sir, I saw a pair of green eyes like those of a dragon, glowing in the dark. But it was a man who ran away." The wide-eyed sentry trembled. "He didn't have wings but he seemed to almost fly, he ran to the dragons, jumped on one and they all flew away."

"All the dragons?"

"Yes sir, they broke their tethers and took off. We couldn't have stopped them, even if we'd been right there."

Onfroi had not foreseen this blow. For ten long years he had planned and schemed. Day and night, he had worked—his goal finally neared to fruition. Now the dragons had escaped and had taken his advantage with them. Dragons didn't defend the castle and the dragon riders in his force would possibly have been the difference between a short battle with a conclusive victory and a long drawn out battle against a well-trained enemy. He didn't have enough men for a lengthy conflict. It angered him that so few had volunteered to join his private army, even with the promise of two meals a day, a warm dry bed at night, and a purse of coins when the war ended. He'd had to exercise caution; he couldn't advertise right under the nose of the King, most of the recruits came from Esterhaven and the far-flung provinces. Those from King's Port itself were the sons of men Onfroi knew he could trust.

Aldus, a picture of affronted, white-faced fury, vented his frustration. Having lost both a bride and a dragon in the past year proved more embarrassment than he could stand. He had relished in the prospect of taking control of the kingdom and the power he would wield. All his life, Aldus had had his every need catered for and he hated to lose. His boot found the rump of a scrawny cur sniffing around for scraps and it yelped away into the night. Onfroi's shiny new battle helm felt his son's boot too; it clanked across the muddy ground and came to rest in a puddle. Dirty water trickled down and pooled in the dent on its crown.

# 23

Ryall read a scroll he had borrowed from his friend, Zildyr and lounged in his favourite chair, his feet rested on the andiron. The crackling flames licked his bare toes. He tried to focus on the words before him as Aalys gnome-jousted with Gnoptly, their Gigag gardener; a simple form of the sport—he attempted to hit her with a hickory stick and she strove to avoid his blows.

"Behold! A fine clout! Yarken to quetch!" Spirited encouragement from the housekeeper, Gniwas, and the cook, Gnohog, messed with Ryall's concentration.

"Nary dringle, Miss Aalys!" Gniwas's voice rose with her excitement. "Frush! Graff yon gundygut with thine sceaft!"

"Hoful—hoful."

"Gofe that hufty-tufty!"

Gnoptly, Gnohog, and Gniwis were Gigags, a race of giant gnomes native to the Isle of L'Áscarle a few miles west of Dorcliff, across the Strait of Glimuth. As tall, but heavier than their human counterparts, they had proportionally shorter legs and longer arms. Their strong-boned faces featured a big nose and large brown eyes.

Ryall and Aalys were the Raigon-talth of Dorcliff Island and until a few months ago, believed themselves the only two of their kind. They celebrated into the night when a missive from Raulin of King's Port announced the long-awaited third Raigon-talth.

The Raigon-talth lived in Tregaryon Hall, a sprawling building of stone and wood high on the cliffs of the southernmost tip of the island. They coexisted peacefully with the Dragons but their Wyvern Emperor, Gernellian the Oppressor, barely tolerated the human element of his kingdom, especially since those humans held a close bond with the dragons. His tolerance declined with each passing year.

Eighty-nine years old, Ryall looked thirty. Tall, with jet-black hair and the bright green eyes, he hailed from Serasya—the Misty Isle—but hadn't spent more than a few hours in his homeland for many years. He hated his King, Guidyon di Dyum of Serasya. He hated Emperor Gernellian (the Golden Wyvern of Dorcliff) even more. He avoided the irritating Slokks of Belcliff. He hadn't been fond of the late King Eustace of Oldegoth either. He hadn't yet encountered the new King, Raulin the Redeemer, Ryall hadn't travelled to King's Port since the crown changed hands. He had speculated why the people called him the redeemer; an epithet likely granted by sycophants but when the bird arrived from Raulin to announce the rise of the third Raigon-talth, Ryall conceded he might have misjudged the new King. The scroll bore the royal seal but he hadn't signed it with his title, rather, *'Kind regards, Raulin.'*

Aalys also hailed from the Misty Isle. Unusually tall, like Ryall, with bright emerald eyes. Her jet-black hair had a patch of white on one side. Twenty-five, Aalys had been a Raigon-talth for five years. Gernellian had killed her predecessor two years before she received the scratch that gave her, her venin blood. Her jollity contrasted with Ryall's querulous disposition; nevertheless, they had an amicable relationship. Their dragon blood gave them keen senses, super-human prowess in strength, speed, and agility.

Ryall pondered how long before the young Raigon-talth would arrive. King Raulin had given him a mission to spy on an enemy of Oldegoth. It exasperated Ryall that the Kingdom of Oldegoth would treat this valuable being with such casual regard and send him on an errand anyone with a bit of nous could fulfil. Earlier that evening, Ryall and Aalys sent telepathic messages to the dragons of Oldegoth to bring the Raigon-talth to Dorcliff Island as soon as a chance presented itself. They doubted the message would reach those dragons whose minds had closed with years of domestication but hoped it would reach some.

It irritated Ryall that no one could decipher the ambiguous and fragmented prophecy. While scholars debated its significance, it fell to Ryall to train the boy and make him worthy of his venin blood. While the training he had received with the Oldegoth King's Elite Guard would hold him in good stead, the Raigon-talth required many more skills than physical combat.

The Raigon-talth and their Gigag servants started; in the adjoining dragon hall, their dragons, Lymelzia and Ryzolth schrieked to the night.

*'The Venin Born approaches! Raigon-talth!'*

*'The enslaved dragons of Oldegoth have broken free. Many hundreds carry a precious burden!'*

*'They bring the Venin Born! Eric Man-Dragon.'*

*'He comes, Raigon-talth! Dorcliff will rise!'*

*'Rise!'*

*'Dragons of Dorcliff, freedom is yours for—'*

"Quiet, fools!" Ryall leapt to his feet. *'Quiet! Do you want Gernellian on our doorstep?'*

He, Aalys, and their Gigag servants hurried to the wide flagged courtyard, searching the night sky. Many dragons approached in the darkness across the Parinith Strait, though unseen, Ryall could hear their thoughts. At the head of the pack, he sensed an unhealthy blend of potency, purity, and recklessness.

*Who is this dragon? Or is it the Raigon-talth on its back?*

"Ryall?" Aalys stepped back and shielded her face. "What—"

A whuff of air buffeted them and two enormous wings spread wide, a green dragon skidded across the flagstones. He rose on his hind legs and screeched to the night sky, white and green flames roared into the air. The Raigon-talth landed weightless before them.

"Show off." Aalys exhaled.

Ryall studied the youth. *Just a boy—a very tall boy.*

"Hello, I'm Eric." He grinned and bowed. "And this is Isuthiel." Hundreds of dragons alit behind them, down the bluff and on the headland. "We've brought a few friends."

"A few? Are there any dragons left in Oldegoth, at all?" Ryall couldn't see all the dragons that landed in the dark, wherever they found a space but the elder Raigon-talth estimated the dragon population of Dorcliff Island had just quintupled, at least.

"I guess only those happy with their human master remain. These came from all over the Kingdom." He gestured behind him and shrugged. "Sorry, I thought only those where I was, were coming. I didn't know until we were half way here that so many followed." Eric's mouth twitched.

"How old are you boy?" Ryall's brow creased, this kid could be a great leader—or perhaps he might destabilise Eald D'Árian.

"Um, fifteen I think, sir."

"You think? Don't you know when you were born?"

"I don't know what year, but it was the winter solstice. It's hard to know when you're growing up on the street." He grinned and looked around at Aalys. His eyes moved to lock on the Gigags; Ryall guessed he had never seen such beings before.

"My name is Ryall, this is Aalys and these are our servants, Gnoptly, Gnohog, and Gniwas. They are Gigags."

The youth before him disturbed Ryall. He seemed unaware of the significance of his Venin blood. Careless and nonchalant, as if on an outing with friends, goofing about. He radiated power; Ryall sensed the potency of his Venin blood suspended in the air around them. "Well, you better come inside. I'm guessing you're hungry."

"Um, yes I am rather, if you have some leftovers or something, I would be most grateful." He licked his lips. "Sir, I must get a message to King Raulin."

"Certainly, come we'll compose the missive and send a bird."

"A bird?"

"Yes, homing pigeons. We exchange pigeons with Castle Greycliff and other cities of Eald D'Árian."

"How?"

"We send them in a cage by ship and Castle Greycliff sends us some of theirs. We have the same arrangement with King Gnogoly of L'Áscarle and with the King of Serasya. As soon as they're released, they fly to their home loft."

**************

"A bowl of clotterpot and a cob of brod for thee, Master Eric." Gnohog set a bowl in front of the newcomer. "May I glosh thee a jubbe of blashy?"

"Um—"

"He means would you like some ale." Ryall's mouth twitched, after many years of listening to the antiquated speech of the Gigags he sometimes caught himself using their words.

"Oh, yes. Thank you." The boy gazed after Gnohog as he stumped back to the kitchen.

**************

"So where were you scratched?"

Ryall had repressed a smile when Aalys propped her elbows on the table to watched Eric eat the large bowl of Gnohog's stew and a sizable chunk of bread. They didn't have much contact with the outside world here on the southern-most headland of Dorcliff. She contained her curiosity long enough for the boy to finish his meal.

"Scratched?" Eric sipped from his mug of ale.

"You know—where the hatchling scratched you, to give you your Venin blood?"

"Oh!" Eric bared the back of his hand, "There. That was the first one." He pulled back the sleeve of his cloak. "Then here, and here." He pulled up his other sleeve,

122

"and here, here, and there. There were a few smaller ones but the scars have faded."

Disbelief etched across Aalys's face.

Ryall strode from the fire. "Show me!"

His lower lip clamped between his teeth, Eric pointed out the raised, pale scars.

Ryall swore quietly. "Well that would explain—"

"I thought that was how all Raigon-talth came to be, by being scratched by a dragon hatchling."

Aalys shook her head. "Only one small scratch. Not– how many? You should be dead!"

"Yes, most people, when scratched by a hatchling, keep away so they don't get scratched again." Ryall examined the scars. "Never has there been a Raigon-talth so richly infused. I'll expect great things from you, young Eric." *How, in the name of Gyarie, The Goddess of Serasya, are we to contain this man-dragon?*

# 24

The pigeon sped through the mist across the Parinith Strait, yearning for its home loft. The lights of King's Port flickered in the predawn and the castle of King Raulin loomed high above the charcoal sea. The bird settled on the stone windowsill and ruffled its feathers. A hand grasped it and slipped the knot that secured the parchment to its leg. The bird cooed gratefully when the man set it in its coop.

"Hm. His Majestys must not receive that intelligence." The loft brightened as the parchment flared and burned over a candle.

**************

With the morning sun at their back, Onfroi and Aldus reigned their horses before their militia. A motley band of peasants, Onfroi held his breath and wished for a change in wind direction.

"Men of Oldegoth!" Onfroi glared at the dirty faces before him. "Tonight we shall make history!"

"Wot's 'istory?" A dull-eyed youth in the front line squinted.

"Might be his story but it ain't my sto—" The scrawny, grey-haired serf stopped, the chortles around him whickered to a halt. When Aldus curled his lip and flexed his lash, the men knew to keep quiet and above all, be serious. In a week's space, their numbers had dropped as men fled Aldus's whip. Since the dragons had deserted camp, Aldus's temperament had soured to the roughest vinegar.

"Tonight we depose King Raulin, the weakest king that Oldegoth has seen in many generations. Tonight we elevate Oldgoth to the most powerful kingdom in all of Eald D'Árian!"

A smatter of applause greeted this prediction.

"Tonight we shall restore prosperity to our people!"

The youth once again vented his curious spleen. "Wot's prosperity?"

Onfroi cut off the snarl that issued from Aldus's clenched teeth. "There is roast venison and potatoes for all, make your way to the cook's wagon. Eat, men of Oldegoth. Then rest and ready your weapons!"

**************

Randolf slipped into the shadows and made his way past the greenhouses. He found the man he sought behind the stables.

"How many have you got?"

"Five of them are prepared to swear allegiance, your Highness. I haven't dared approach the rest; I'd like to keep my head on my shoulders."

"So who does that leave?"

"Gilda, of course. Haman, Nalfar, Clarice, Derrin and seven others. The Raigon-talth has been gone for a week and Gilda is not saying where he is."

"Well, if and when he does return he is to be arrested and thrown into the dungeons with the others." Randolf checked up and down the narrow alley where they stood. Silence blanketed the castle in the dead of night. The lighthouse lit the towers with a ghostly flicker but in the alley where he stood, darkness reigned. An owl hooted inside the stable.

"When can we expect Lord Onfroi to arrive?" asked Tomas.

"Two nights hence—I cannot give you an exact time. You and your men must be ready. Remember, I don't want anyone killed, especially the King."

"We may have to kill those of the Elite Guard, you know we swear to protect the King with our lives, we vow to fight to our death."

"I said I don't want them killed, Tomas."

"And I'm saying we might not have a choice! You're hoping for too much, your Highness, if you think we can stage a bloodless coup."

"Hm." Randolf clenched his fists. "And what of Sir Cesper? Were you able to ascertain whose side he will take?"

"I afraid Cesper is very much his own man and he has unswerving loyalty from his knights—"

"I told you to sound him out—who would he support in a hypothetical coup."

"I did. He says he is always loyal to Oldegoth."

"Damn him!"

# 25

Larkin tilted his head to gaze at the beautiful, dark-haired girl that carried his dinner tray.

"Please, join me?" He dazzled her with a smile and rejoiced when her cheeks turned pink. "I hate to eat alone and Milo isn't as pretty as you. Please? You have finished your duties, have you not?"

"Very well, I'll fetch another plate." Her scent lingered as she turned back to the kitchen.

"And bring another glass? I should tell you, I also hate to drink alone."

Larkin was in love. The strange new emotions that afflicted him since Cateline had arrived in his household could only be love. He'd never felt this way before and he wasn't sure he liked it. Since he'd arrived in the Kingdom of Oldegoth he'd lived in his little utopia—a voluntary prisoner in a foreign land. He answered to himself, except occasionally when Milo required his attention. He earned a comfortable living riding Telzoth each week at the Coliseum. He had four close friends, Milo, Calder, Raulin, and Gilda—until recently when he befriended Eric and his sister, Cateline. Cateline had rattled his gilded cage. It hadn't occurred to him that he might meet a girl he'd want to marry. His father had betrothed him to the daughter of an aristocrat though given his self-imposed exile fourteen years before, Larkin doubted that betrothal still held. Would marriage to Cateline complicate things? Given who he was, did it bear consideration?

For Larkin wasn't just Larkin. He was Crown Prince Guidyon di Larkyn, heir to the throne of Serasya. His home lay across the sea, in Asyann, the capital city of Serasya—the Misty Isles. Would his father, King Guidyon di Dyum the Peeved, in the absence of his elder son, pass the crown to his younger son Prince Guidyon di Elyot the Cripple? Larkin worried his father's desire for more land might prove the doom of Serasya.

Memories danced across unseeing eyes, dazzled by the candle flame before him. His mind meandered to that boyhood day as he soared on Telzoth, high above the fiery Brimstone Archipelago, boiling in the Sea of Serasya, creating the steam that gave his country its other name, The Misty Isles. On the northern bluffs of Dorcliff Island, he sighted broken pillars standing among rubble—the ruins of the fabled Golden Hall of Serasya. The discovery had allowed him, in his innocence, to complete the map his father needed to find the one he believed would grant him power to rule the world of Eald D'Árian. Warmly congratulated for his keen eye, Prince Guidyon di Larkyn rejoiced; it took much to impress his father. King Guidyon Di Dyum's dream shone real when his son pinpointed the legendary ruins of Golden Hall of Serasya on the map.

*"You've done me proud, son—now I can free Inigo Thornfingers. My reward will be power to rule all the lands of Eald D'Árian."*

*"But how do you know He will give you this power, father?"* The boy Prince studied the pinched faced of his father.

*"He is all powerful—the one who frees Him will be richly rewarded."*

*"But the Gigags locked Him in there; won't they try and stop you freeing Him?"*

*"Been reading your history, have you Prince Larkyn?"*

*"Yes father."*

Young Prince Larkyn had worried for his people, he feared that if roused to war, the Gigags of L'Áscarle would make a formidable enemy. If allied with their neighbours, the Slokks of Bellcliff Island, no army could stop them. For many years, the Slokks threatened to restrict movement through the Dorcliff Channel—the sole ship's passage out of the circular archipelago and the life-giving trade route to the Kingdom of Serasya. Young Guidyon Di Larkyn understood the Gigags were peacekeepers of the Archipelago. Something his father failed to grasp; instead, he dreamed he'd drive the Gigags and the Slokks from their island homes, and seize the abundant farmlands of Oldegoth. Serasya lay high on the globe, shrouded in mist and food crops impossible. Its wealth dwelled under the rocky surface, the people mined vast mineral wealth to trade with Oldegoth for food and fibre—a position the King of Serasya considered untenable; an enemy could easily starve a country unable to grow food. Guidion di Dyum's take on international diplomacy had two core beliefs. If you want it—take it. If you don't like it—kill it.

Weeks of careful consideration and long conversations with Zylder, his personal tutor, the prince had acted. In the middle of the night, Prince Guidyon di Larkyn crept into his father's private study and stole the map. He had slipped past the guards, mounted Telzoth and at the age of twelve, he left the Kingdom of Serasya. He could not imagine a time when he would return. He carried a scroll Zylder gave him, addressed to Milo, Wizard of the Order of St Alúthien, in the city of King's Port.

Cateline's light footsteps broke his reverie. Larkin rose, drew out a chair and held her hand as she sat down.

"You are too beautiful to be a housekeeper, Cateline. I'm taking steps to find someone else for that task."

Her blue eyes widened and worry stole across her dainty face.

"Do not worry," he raised her hand to his lips. "You are not going anywhere."

Larkin and Cateline started as the dragons screeched in their stable. He and Milo reached the back door together.

"What is it?"

"I don't know."

They grabbed torches off the wall and dashed into the dark but found nothing; Larkin regretted his inability to talk to dragons. Their ruffled scales showed their agitation; Telzoth poked his head through the window and roared flames into the darkness. Larkin and Milo wandered about in the dark with torches but found nothing. The dragons paced around, hissing.

Back in the dining room, Larkin's heart dropped to his stomach. A plate of food lay smashed across the floor.

"Cateline?"

Larkin ran to the kitchen, to the parlour then to Cateline's bedroom. She had vanished. His shaking hands snatched up the small brass bell and shook it; Milo hurried in.

"Larkin, have you found something?"

"I cannot find Cateline—" His gaze fell upon a scroll on the floor, under a chair.

*'You have three whole days to return what you stole. If you should fail, your woman will die.'* Larkin stared at the seal of King Guidion di Dyum. He believed the words before him—well aware of his father's capacity for cold-blooded murder.

"So he has given up on diplomacy."

# 26

Luphil lounged at his post, his finger explored his left nostril and he chewed a piece of jerky. The barn owl hooted down at the stables as it did every night. A freezing wind blew in from the Parinith Strait. He hunkered down behind the wall, pulled his cowl tighter and waited for the bell to toll three times. When it did, he could go to his warm bed. He grew drowsy; it was almost warm down here out of the wind.

He woke to a sharp point against his chest.

"If you want to live, stay quiet." A man loomed over him and the spear point spiked the skin over his heart; Luphil raised his hands. The clatter of boots on stone echoed in the dark, past the gatehouse, through the streets and up towards the King's tower.

**************

Gilda woke to the ringing of bells. She flung back the covers, leapt to her feet and dressed, sword in hand she ran down the stairs.

"Go back to your quarters, Gilda."

She stopped, unsure of Tomas's motive.

"Why are the bells ringing?"

Tomas advanced, sword raised. Clarice, Haman, Nalfar, and Derrin halted beside Gilda.

"What's the trouble, Tomas?" Haman's voice wary as his head turned, scanning the room; more of the Elite Guard joined them, weapons drawn.

"Go back to your quarters all of you."

"Those bells mean the King is in danger, stop messing around, Tomas!"

Tomas placed the tip of his sword against Gilda's throat. "I am not messing around." The quiet malevolence in his voice prickled down Gilda's spine. "I said go back to your quarters and stay there!"

Gilda swung her sword up and parried Tomas's blade. The Tower of the Guard erupted with shouts, clanging blades and the clack of quarterstaffs.

**************

Clarice moved to Gilda's side, her eyes fixed on Teiry, a man who had joined the Elite Guard only months before her.

"Why are you doing this?"

"Oldegoth shall have a new King."

"Over my dead body!" Haman's staff swished past Clarice's head and smashed the sword from a traitor's fingers.

Clarice whipped around to clash steel with Teiry. Her blade held level with her nose as the Elite Guard had taught her. She stalled Teiry's strike but a grin curled his lips as her sword shivered under his brutal strength.

"Weapons nary belong in the hands of a little girl." He pressed closer, the blade flashed and hummed as he swung; the torch's reflection danced over the cool steel.

Clarice ducked and swung blindly, her blade sliced through muscle and bone. A spray of blood splashed her feet as she dragged her sword from Teiry's chest, certain he'd breathed his last. She screamed in terror as blood sprayed from Gilda's throat, the captain of the Elite Guard swung her final blow for The King and Tomas's head parted his shoulders. Gilda fell in a pool of blood, her eyes stared, unseeing at the ceiling. Clarice fell to her knees and tears fell on her cheeks. King Raulin's greatest warrior lay dead.

The invaders' feet slipped on the bloody stone as they surrounded those faithful to Raulin and marched them to the dungeon.

**************

At the door of the King's Tower, four Elite Guardsmen listen to the distant sounds of fighting. Along the hall came the familiar clunk and scrape as Nutley approached with surprising speed. A ring of iron keys jingled on his sash.

He wheezed to a halt and snivelled. "Skullduggery has awoken! We must move the King!"

The Elite Guardsmen drew their swords. "Yes! Quickly! Move him to The Keep and lock him in. The castle has been breached!"

"It has."

"Hurry, Nutley. We'll meet them head on."

"Fight bravely, Gentlemen."

"And Nutley, when the King is safe, disappear. The King's life may depend on you—you'll know what to do."

**************

Nutley pulled Raulin through the darkness by the hem of his nightshirt. "Quickly, your Majesty! This way. Quickly—to the Keep—evil is afoot."

"Where is Calder?"

"He was summoned to Master Larkin's house, your Majesty and he hasn't returned. My first priority is to get you to safety, only then will I search for Calder."

Shouts, clangs, and crashes of combat reached Raulin's ears.

"Who is attacking us, Nutley?"

*Need I ask?*

"That treasonous devil-scum, Onfroi, and his army of traitors." Nutley spat on the stones and wheezed with exertion as he pulled Raulin up the stairs; his hickory staff clunked on the stones, his sandals scraped and shuffled. "He seeks to raise his son to the throne. Your inner circle has traitors and many heads must roll, Sire. Now bolt this door from the inside your Majesty, when it is safe I will come for you." Nutley shoved Raulin into the Keep and pulled the heavy iron door closed. A loud click told Raulin, Nutley had locked him in.

"Where are the knights, Nutley?"

Nutley didn't answer.

Raulin shot the iron bolts home.

# 27

Ryall and Aalys began training Eric at daybreak, what he'd learned with the Elite Guard held him in good stead for the physical combat and weaponry. They progressed quickly on to telepathic communication.

"I have no problem communicating with dragons."

"Of course you don't, you're a Raigon-talth and you'll have little problem communicating with Aalys and I." Ryall made himself comfortable by the fire. "What you have to learn is how to break in to a closed mind."

As predicted, Eric had no problem communicating telepathically with Ryall and Aalys. Breaking into their thoughts while they resisted the intrusion gave him headaches. After several hours, he managed to penetrate Aalys's mind, but Ryall's left Eric exhausted.

"I feel like I've been trampled by a blaze of dragons."

Ryall frowned. "I'm not finished with you yet."

Ryall ordered him to intrude into Gnoptly's mind and Eric collapsed at first try.

"What—" Eric sat up, "what happened?"

"Thou must prevail most potently if ye wish to breach thee wits of a Gigag." Gnoptly wheezed and bared his big teeth in a magnificent Gigag grin.

"Get up and try again!" Ryall scowled. "Gnoptly is trained to resist you; you'll have to try harder."

Eric scrambled upright and concentrated on the Gigag, *'Gnoptly'* A purple flash temporarily blinded him and knocked him back to the ground.

Ryall pulled him to his feet. "Use your mind like an axe."

Eric shook his head. He might have run into a wall.

He made a mental lunge at the Gigag's mind.

*'Gnoptly—'* He caught the tail end of his thoughts then reeled from a telepathic punch. Gnoptly's eyes widened.

"I need a drink." Eric strolled to the table and poured a cup of water. He sighed and raised it to his mouth.

*'Gnoptly!'* He mentally rammed a foot in the door of the Gigag's mind.

*'He nearly frushed me that ti— Ah! Out with ye!'*

*'Hello Gnoptly, I got you this time.'* Gnoptly shoved with his mind but Eric dug deeper. Slivers of memories flickered before him—digging in the garden—picking runner beans; an elderly Gigag laughed and raised a tankard. A female Gigag ; her eyes widened...

*'Ye be better than aught I imagined, Master Eric,'* Gnoptly didn't seem to mind that Eric had invaded his mind, *'now begone! I say, afore ye ogle things nowt for beholding with thine child's eyes!'*

Eric laughed and Gnoptly mentally shoved him.

Ryall's brow creased. "Stay calm! Such human emotions as laughing will make the connection weak. They'll force you out if you laugh or cry or become angry. A trained enemy will also invade if your mind is weakened by emotions. You must stay perfectly calm!"

"Oh he breached me that time, Master Ryall!" Gnoptly chuckled. "Snuck up on me!" He shook his head, laughter rumbled in his thick neck.

Eric gazed after him as he stomped out to the garden. "So the Gigags can speak to dragons too?"

"No. Not unless they become Raigon-talth."

"They can become—"

"Yes, if they survive the scratch of a dragon hatchling."

"Have there ever been any?"

"I believe so. Yes, though never in my time." Ryall sat at the table and stretched his legs. "You should manage to communicate with all creatures that are reasonably intelligent, though they may not relate back, not telepathically, anyway. They might respond to a suggestion."

Eric's favourite past time at Tregaryon hall was Gnome Jousting, although unlike Aalys, Eric jousted with all three of the Gigag servants at once. Hours of practice, numerous lumps and bruises later, the Gigags admitted defeat, unable to land a blow on the youngest Raigon-talth.

# 28

Larkin ran to the door as it shook under a pounding fist. He wrenched it open to Basil, the head of the City Watch.

"What—"

"Come quickly, Larkin—a distressed young lady is asking for you."

"Cateline?"

"I believe that is her name."

"Take me to her."

The danger of the sulky capsizing never entered Larkin's head as he clung to the seat beside Basil and worried what might have befallen Cateline. The sulky jerked to a halt and Larkin's feet found the pavement behind Basil.

"This way, Larkin."

Through the gaol house, along the dark, stone-flagged passage to the cells, Larkin trailed Basil. In the gloom of an open cell, a woman lay facing the wall.

"Cateline!" He hurried to her. As the woman turned to face him, the cell door clanged and Basil vanished. "Cateline?"

"Sorry, Lovie. Cateline ain't 'ear. Basil!" The woman bawled after Basil then bared her brown teeth at

Larkin. "A girl 'as to earn a livin' and this is the easiest florin I ever earnt."

"Where is Cateline?"

"Dunno." She vented her tonsils again. "Basil! You bespawling dalcop! Come back here and pay up!"

"This is—"

"Yeah, sorry lovie—Basil! Let me out now, you gillie-wet-footed wandought!"

Long hours laboured by, morning passed into midday and wore on to late afternoon. The Crown Prince of Serasya fretted and paced the tiny cell listening as the woman cast aspersions on Basil's ancestry, personal hygiene, and intellect. Through his worry and weariness, part of Larkin marvelled at her tenacity and lungpower.

Finally, an hour after sundown, Basil reappeared.

"Basil! You miserable piece of horse—"

"Shut up, Mertle! If you want to get out today, shut up." Basil unlocked the cell and pulled the door open. Mertle shoved through and extended her grubby hand to receive a silver coin.

Larkin seized Basil's shirtfront and shoved him against the bars.

"What have you done with Cateline?"

"I know nothing about what happened to your Cateline—for all I know she might be blind drunk and dancing with a sailor at the tavern."

The bars rang like collision bells as Larkin knocked Basil's head against it. "If anything has happened to that girl, I'll be back here and you'll be sorry!" Larkin kicked him into the cell, locked it and removed the key.

"Give me those keys or I'll have you arrested!"

"You'll need to catch me first, no?" Larkin shook the keys at Basil and dropped them into a chamber pot fermenting in the corridor.

"Things is gonna change around this city, Larkin—we have a new King—King Randolf! Raulin the Redeemer is locked in The Keep, Gilda and half the Elite Guard are dead; the rest are locked in the dungeon!" Basil's portends dogged him along the corridor. "And you can forget about the Wizards, they've all gone into hiding! Your dragon…"

Fear pulsed in Larkin's throat as he sprinted back to his manor, he would take Telzoth and fly across the sea to Asyann, the city of his birth. He had long ago burned the map to the Golden Hall of Serasya but he could easily pinpoint it on another. The doors of the dragon hall stood open and the stalls empty.

"Telzoth?"

Into his manor he crashed. "Milo!" He leaned against the wall trying to catch his breath. "Milo!"

The empty house answered with silence.

**************

On his seventh try, Larkin found a ship's captain, who dared speak to him.

"I'm sorry to say, Mr Larkin, but Basil has closed the harbour entrance to all outbound ships. I cannot take you anywhere." The man looked around and lowered his voice. "If I were you, I'd get out of this city. Basil has ordered your arrest—assault and damage to crown property—what did you damage?"

"Basil—and I'll do it again, no?"

The Captain tossed him a piece of hopsack. "Cover your Serasyan blond head, Larkin—your enemies could spot it in the dark from a hundred yards. Good luck." The Captain disappeared up the gangway.

Larkin tried to quell his rising panic. He hurried back to Mystmere and up to the pigeon loft. Thirty-six hours had passed; without a dragon, he had little chance of rescuing Cateline. He trusted his hopes to Eric, dashed off a quick note and tied it to a pigeon. As the bird fluttered into the night, Larkin silently thanked Raulin who had insisted he take a Raigon-talth's pigeon in case Cateline wanted to contact her brother.

**************

Onfroi hadn't foreseen the disapproval that greeted his new regime. The population of King's Port dwindled. Overnight, many of the citizens had packed up and left. Others loaded their possessions into carts, ready to flee. To counter the exodus, he had set Aldus and a handful of men to guard Castle Greycliff; the rest of his forces he sent to guard the perimeter of the city.

"Nobody leaves, do I make myself clear?"

"Yessir."

"Awright, sir."

A day later, a knock on his manor door brought him from his bed before dawn. He opened it to a bullnecked man with a wild tangle of blond curls.

"What do you want at this ungodly hour, Ramsey?"

Ramsey gulped and looked at his feet. "Sir, we fear something is amiss in the city, sir."

"Your only order was to stop people leaving the city, what could be amiss?"

"People are afraid, sir. While Basil and his men are busy watching the ships in the harbour, evil is stalking the streets."

"Evil—what are you talking about, man?"

"A spectre, cloaked in black has been seen peering through windows and several families have had children taken in the middle of the night. They fear Tagrali—"

"Get back to your post, Ramsey! You're a grown man, too old to believe in ghost stories."

"But sir, people have—"

"Back to your post! Now!" Onfroi slammed the door and marched to the kitchen. "Elspeth! Serve me my breakfast! Immediately!"

# 29

The pigeon fluttered in the shaft of morning sun streaming through the open door. Its wings wafted the air and whorls of dust shimmered in the golden light. Ryall enjoyed the sun's fragile warmth and sipped a mug of tea. The pigeon alit on the arm of his chair and cooed. Ryall removed the missive attached to its leg and thrust the bird at Aalys.

"See this bird is safely caged and fed."

Ryall's frown had deepened to a scowl by the time Aalys returned.

"Bad tidings?"

"Where's Eric?"

"I think he took Isuthiel for a flight."

"Here I am." Eric entered the room from the dragon hall.

"Your sister is missing."

"My sister—missing—how?" The lines of Eric's body stiffened and his faced blanched.

Ryall read aloud. *"Please advise Eric that his sister Cateline, has been kidnapped. Regards, Larkin.'* Who is this Larkin?"

"He's a Dragon Ace, my sister works for him."

"He didn't give us much information. Who would be kidnapping your sister?"

"There's only one person I can think of who would do that, but how did he find her?" Eric told them about Onfroi and his son Aldus.

"There is a way we can see where she is." Aalys took the chair beside Ryall. "You'll have to allow us to see into your mind so we know what she looks like, then we may be able to scry her."

"How does that work?"

"Picture your sister in your mind."

***************

Eric easily called on a memory of the last time he had seen Cateline in Larkin's kitchen, talking and laughing. He felt Aalys and Ryall push into the scene and examine his sister.

"Right! Pretty girl." Eric inhaled as Ryall withdrew from his mind. "Now we must try to scry her. We find her, concentrate on her and try to see her thoughts."

***************

Fifteen minutes later, they gathered around the table discussing what they had seen. They had found Cateline in a dimly lit room; the floor and walls constructed from grey stone, furnished with a narrow bed, a wooden chair and table. A single candle burned in a small, stone bowl. Her tear-blurred gaze had revealed a barred window and beyond, a cityscape cloaked in fog—vague outlines of steep streets and buildings nestled into the mountainside. High above the city, the mountain reached toward the firmament; white streams of water tumbled down its rocky flanks and wended their way under arched bridges, along deep gullies and into the sea.

"I'm sure what we saw is Asyann." Aalys rested her elbows on the table.

"Where's Asyann?" Eric jiggled his foot; calmly discussing what they'd observed while his sister faced danger unsettled him. He wanted to search for her.

"Asyann is the capital of Serasya."

"Serasya? Oh yes, I've heard of it."

"Some of your people call it the Misty Isles—some call it The Invisible Kingdom. Serasya is almost always shrouded in fog."

"Why would she be there?" Eric shook his head, grappling with myriad thoughts that battered his brain. What incriminating secret did Randolf know about Larkin? "Why would he kidnap her? No, he wouldn't—that's just stupid. And why would he send her to Asyann? I wish I knew more about him."

Aalys shook her head. "Who?"

"Larkin."

Ryall frowned and scratched his head. "How long have you known him?"

"Not that long, less than six months. He seems like a good man, although—" What he'd overheard while eavesdropping on Onfroi's tent kept niggling.

"Although?"

Eric related the conversation between Onfroi and Randolf. While Eric spoke of Larkin, he sensed Ryall push into his mind again. Eric showed him a memory of the Dragon Ace. He had a sense of Ryall having a quick search around through Eric's recollections of Larkin and then the elder Raigon-talth withdrew sharply.

"What—"

Ryall flung up a hand to silence his companions. His face went still, his eyes shut against his surroundings. Eric glanced at Aalys who watched Ryall closely, her eyes flicked to Eric's and she shook her head.

A minute ticked slowly then Ryall exploded to his feet. He strode out the door and stood breathing the cool morning air, lost in his thoughts.

"What did you see?" Aalys shot the question after him, one Eric hadn't dared voice.

"I'm not sure." Ryall's voice held a quaver; Eric thought he sounded apprehensive.

Eric and Aalys locked gazes but neither spoke. Ryall resumed his seat and once again went into the trance-like state. Ten minutes later, Eric contemplated giving him a shake to see if he slept; Ryall opened his eyes and jumped to his feet.

"The heir to the throne of Serasya!" The younger Raigon-talth stared at their elder. "The long lost heir. I'm sure of it! Dragon Ace Larkin is Crown Prince Guidyon di Larkyn. He's hiding in a cave and he's grieving for the loss of a dear friend, I entered his mind easily." Ryall gazed at the floor. "His wizard would have trained him to keep me out but he's let his guard down. He fears for the life of your sister whom he is deeply in love with. He fears for the future of all in Eald Arián. Eric, we need to scry King Raulin."

"How is this going to help my sister?"

"We need to know why she's been kidnapped, although I'm starting to form an idea in my mind as to who is holding her and what their motives are."

"But—can't we just—" Eric's fists clenched.

"We'll get your sister back, Eric! But we need to know what King Raulin is doing and then we'll look into what King Guidyon di Dyum is up to. He's obviously found where the Prince fled to, but what does he want from him? King Dyum is a harsh ruler—even his sons would not be immune to his tyranny."

Fear prickled down Eric's spine. "Who is Larkin grieving for?"

"A woman." Ryall opened his mind and allowed Eric to see Larkin's thoughts still fresh in his mind.

"Gilda." Eric felt the tears rise in his eyes, *Please, not Gilda.* "If Gilda is dead then King Raulin may be dead too." *And Clarice.* Anger boiled in Eric's chest.

"Eric, calm down. Relax your mind. Do it—relax! Now show me King Raulin, please?"

Eric inhaled a long breath and pictured King Raulin. Ryall entered Eric's mind then withdrew. His face relaxed a moment then he jumped, his eyes opened in surprise.

"Your King packs a punch. No, he's not dead. I think he's in a dungeon."

"What else did you find out?"

"Nothing, as soon as he realised I was scrying him, he kicked me out. The wizards have trained him well."

"Okay, then scry this mongrel." Eric conjured a mental picture of Randolf.

Again Ryall relaxed and scried. After a few minutes, he opened his eyes and shook his head, "It's hard to make sense of the thoughts of a man who has just polished off most of the King's personal wine collection. He's deep in his cups and he is not a happy man, even though he is wearing the crown."

"Curse him!"

"It would seem his friend, Onfroi, is making demands Randolf finds repugnant."

"Let me guess, Onfroi wants a knighthood for he and his son?"

"I don't know—King Randolf's mind is swimming in fine old Gigag wine. Now, let me dig into the foetid bog that is the brain of my King, Guidyon di Dyum the Peeved."

"Peeved?" Eric snorted in spite of his distress.

"It's not his official epithet—it is his nature."

Several minutes later, Ryall once again jumped to his feet and swore.

"It seems Dyum has made some kind of deal with Onfroi. He's holding your sister and demanding Larkin return to Serasya. Larkin has something that Dyum wants badly. If he doesn't get what he wants, your sister will be thrown off the cliffs of Dionisya."

"Where is that?"

"The cliffs of Dionisya are the southern coastline of Asyann. At their highest point they are about two thousand feet above sea level. Larkin has until midday tomorrow."

Eric's stomach churned. "Well, let's go!"

"Wait, Eric—"

"What now?"

**************

*'I've never wanted to kill a human before but I swear on the blood of my dragon forebears, if that filth approaches me again, I'm going to burn the very flesh off his unworthy bones!'* Telzoth paced the length of the heavy, wrought-iron gates that held them captive. Black smoke

chuffed from his mouth and nostrils. Normally relaxed, the spikes on his head and neck stood erect. Tenebrozi's tail twitched, Telzoth spoke of killing a human.

*'We don't need to cook him,'* Azuria timidly pointed out.

Telzoth hulked over Tenebrozi and Azuria. Tenebrozi caught waves of fury and indignation. Telzoth's master had disappeared. Aldus's pretence to have Larkin imprisoned here, had lured the dragons. Anxiety niggled in Tenebrozi's naive mind; Milo had disappeared too. Tenebrozi loved Milo who treated him with apples and kindness.

*'What else can we do?'* His gaze moved from Azuria to the massive sea-green dragon whose chest pulsed with an orange and yellow glow, smoke leaked from his nostrils. Tenebrozi puffed out a thin stream of grey smoke; Telzoth the Magnificent was now, Telzoth the Terrifying.

*'Between us we can melt those bars—'*

Telzoth came to a halt. His talons scored the stones under his feet. *'Melt—yes we can do that.'* Telzoth examined the bars, searching for a weak spot. *'Not the bars, just the catch will do.'*

*'That would make less noise.'* Tenebrozi's tongue flicked over his lips, he didn't want to kill any humans. A noisy escape would bring the humans and Telzoth might kill them. In Tenebrozi's young mind, all humans were kind and good, like Eric, Milo, and Larkin.

*************

Larkin had fallen into a fitful sleep after many hours pacing around in Eric's darkened cavern. Lying on his back in the sand, a sudden shift in the air around him brought him wide-awake.

"Telzoth!" He jumped to his feet. "I am glad to see you! Azuria! Tenebrozi! We have work to do, my friends. We have to find Cateline; she is in Asyann. You remember how to fly there, yes?" He climbed onto Telzoth's enormous shoulders. "Lead the way, Telzoth. Asyann! As fast as your wings can carry us!"

# 30

Eric trembled, anger burned in his guts as he paced the room.

"What are we waiting for?"

"I'm going to try and communicate with Zildyr."

"Who in hell is Zildyr?"

"He is a scholar in Asyann and while he works for the King he isn't afraid to oppose him—frankly, I'm amazed he still has his head."

"Enough! My sister—"

"Eric, calm down!"

Eric had a sense of Ryall drawing his mind to him—a mental hug. Eric flung him off "Let's go—now!"

"Eric, you must calm your anger. Please, it'll get you killed—"

"My sister is in danger! Don't you even care?" The child in him lashed out at Ryall's serenity. He sensed the elder's mind touch his and he shoved him away. "I'm out of here, are you coming with me or not?" Angry tears for Cateline welled in his eyes, his sister—his only family—the thought of losing her terrified the child inside. Since they lost their parents, Cateline had frequently put herself in peril to care for her brother. Now fifteen with the power of a grown man, Eric had failed to protect her.

He ran to the dragon hall, Ryall and Aalys followed.

On the highest point of the Rock of Amycia, Eric sat Isuthiel and gazed across the narrow strait, to the Cliffs of Dionysia. According to the city bells, noon drew close.

Eric had sought to mount an assault on the palace but the King had Cateline heavily guarded. They waited, when the King's men appeared on the cliff they would seize her. He scried his sister; she watched a crippled and twisted man whose face resembled Larkin's. He argued bitterly with an elderly man seated on an ornate silver and gold throne. Cateline's exhausted mind couldn't follow the conversation. Eric sensed the dispute had raged for some time, weasel words chasing pointless and unheeded opinions—around and around and getting nowhere. Finally, the King clapped and six guards appeared.

"You two, take my son away!" He pointed out two guards and they snapped to attention, eyes fixed on the floor. "He's letting his foolish heart rule his head. Lock him in his quarters." The guards dragged the struggling prince away. "You lot, bring the girl. It seems my eldest son doesn't care what happens to his wench. Assemble my knights; if he thinks he can snatch her off the cliffs, he's going to have a fight on his hands. Without a dragon there's not much he can do against forty armed fighting men."

"But he has a dragon, Sire, remember? He took his dragon, Telzoth, with him."

"His dragon has been taken from him. Lord Onfroi of King's Port assures me he has captured three dragons and one of them is Telzoth." Satisfaction glowed on the

King's cruel face. "Onfroi has promised me my elder son will be captured too—an arrest warrant has been issued. He stole from me and he will pay dearly."

Eric pulled out of Cateline's mind and swore bitterly. "Three dragons! That means Onfroi has also captured Azuria and Tenebrozi! Damn!"

*'We'll get them back, Eric.'* Isuthiel's words reassured his anxious mind. *'But we must focus our attention on your sister. We need to be swift, take hold of me, Eric. When your sister is thrown from that cliff we will have only seconds.'*

Aalys called from beside him. "Here they come! See the flags?"

"Yes, I see them," The elder Raigon-talth touched Eric's mind. "Be calm, Eric."

"I am!" Eric's jaw clenched over his words—a clock spring in his mind wound tighter and tighter. Then a sensation of calm enveloped him and soothed the frightened child. "How did you do that?" His extremities warmed, his muscles relaxed; he might have sat before a blazing hearth and not here, at the top of the Rock of Amycia in the thin sleet that blew from the Serasyan Sea.

"Focus your mind, Eric."

Eric exhaled and renewed his grip on the reins.

"Time to fly, my friends!" Ryall's voice carried on the wind and in their thoughts. Isuthiel spread his wings and leapt from the edge; the howling wind buffeted Eric and tugged at his hood. His cloak flapped noisily and freezing droplets stung his face. Ryall's words penetrated his mind. *'Be ready!'*

Eric scried Cateline in brief takes, unable to stay focussed in the chaos of a besieged mind. He took in images of the mist and sleet, blurred by his sister's tears as she reeled from the black rocks of the cliff edge and pled for her life. Far below the grey waves crashed—heard but not seen in the freezing fog, visibility dimmed to a few paces. The gale-force wind howled up the cliff-face; Cateline's hair clung to her face and neck; the wind tugged at her skirt. Men held her arms and forced her forward; wind plucked the screams from her mouth and spirited them away in the mist. Eric withdrew from his sister's thoughts, with his Raigon-talth eyes he watched and seethed as the men marched her to the edge.

**************

King Guidyon di Dyum cursed the swirling mist that obscured the girl; the gale forbade he approach the cliff. The sleet chilled his face—the King longed for the warmth of his carriage.

"Do it!" He shouted to the men who held the struggling, hysterical girl.

The guards forced her to the edge and shoved. Out of the mist a green dragon's head appeared; the knights fired arrows and threw spears. The dragon schrieked and scorched the knights with a jet of white and green fire. Their skin blistered as they hit the ground and rolled to quench the flames. Their screams disembodied in the mist.

*************

A stab of anger distracted Eric; his wild grab caught the fabric of Cateline's skirt. It tore and his sister fell into the mist. A huge green dragon shot below Isuthiel and a shout reached his ears.

"Catch me!"

A fair-haired man dived from the green dragon and Eric saw his arms close around Cateline before they disappeared into the mist. Isuthiel plummeted, Eric's weightless body trailed in the air as he clung to the saddle. Down, Isuthiel dropped and veered as a black dragon sped past, his thrashing wings sprayed water and buffeted the air. The black swooped to catch Cateline and her rescuer. Eric glimpsed the black dragon skim the iron-grey waves and bank at jagged rocks of the cliff base. Eric clambered back into the saddle and Isuthiel's wings pulled them up to the Rock of Amycia.

*'Eric!'* Azuria's voice, sweet and welcoming, greeted him from the mist.

*'Eric!'* Tenebrozi flew on his other side, *'what did you think of my flying? Just now? Have I improved?'*

*'You did well, Tenebrozi!'* Eric held his breath as he strained to see the man on Tenebrozi's back; he twisted in the saddle as a dragon screamed behind him, *'Telzoth?'*

*'Yes, Master Eric. We came for your sister, Cateline. My Master Larkin wants to mate with her. She is precious to him. She is precious to us all.'*

They alighted at the top of the Rock of Amycia; Eric jumped to the ground, Tenebrozi settled gently beside him. White-faced and dishevelled, Larkin's legs fixed around Tenebrozi's shoulders, his arms clutched Cateline. Larkin patted her cheek, his wet hair trickled water down his face.

"Talk to me, Cateline, please—"

Ryall and Aalys landed with a clatter and scratching talons; small pebbles flew and bounced.

"You got her?"

"Larkin got her." Eric jumped off Isuthiel and hurried to examine his sister, his terror for her choked his voice.

Ryall and Aalys dismounted and bowed low, "Your Highness—"

Larkin wasn't listening, "Cateline! Can you hear me? Please Cateline, talk to me."

*'She's unhurt, Eric. Your sister's mind shut down to block the fear.'*

Eric looked at Azuria. *'Shut down? But—'*

"What your dragon means, Eric, is she fainted," Ryall spoke beside him.

Eric reached up, Larkin allowed him to take Cateline's weight, and together, they lowered her to the ground.

"Eric, we have to get out of here!" Ryall searched the surrounding mist. "If this mist lifts—and it could at any minute—the King's men will see us. They have dragons too, you know. Aalys and I drove them back, but we don't want to fight them."

"Eric," Larkin pulled Eric to kneel beside him. "I pray your sister will recover and when she does it is my wish to marry her. Will you give her to me? I'm not good at this, yes? Will you give your permission—?"

"You don't need my permission but you have it anyway—I'm sure my parents would have been pleased—"

Cateline opened her eyes. "Larkin! Eric! What happened?"

"Cateline!" Larkin's arms tightened around her; he pressed his lips to her forehead. "Oh, Cateline! I feared I had lost you!"

"Come, your Highness, you must move, for your own safety!"

"Highness." Larkin looked up and wiped a shaking hand over his face. "It has been many years since anyone called me that. I think I like Larkin better."

# 31

Gnoptly, Gnohog, and Gniwis bowed so low Eric expected grit-tipped noses when they resumed the perpendicular.

"Please," Larkin repeated, "do not make a fuss. I'm happy with whatever you have in the pot, yes?"

"Nay! Thine Kingly appetite demands Kingly crug, not aught auld maw-wallop and clotterpot." Gnohog bared his slab-like teeth. "And thine bellibone lass looms frightfully carked. We can nay expect her to glop fire-fanged crug."

"Well—um—thank you."

Eric grinned at Larkin's confusion, clearly unsure what might land on his plate.

"Let me fillie thee a jubbe of hum, we nay can have the King burstig."

"Thank you, Gnohog." Ryall grinned. "Come and make yourselves comfortable while the staff prepare. Gniwis, can you see the guest rooms are ready?"

"Verily, Master Ryall—thine behests are mine boddles."

**************

Eric and Larkin spent most of the next day monitoring Cateline for signs of distress. She told them of her ordeal, how someone had placed a cloth over her face and the sting of ether in her lungs. She woke, imprisoned in the Royal Palace of Asyann. Larkin's brother, Elyot had tried desperately to have her freed.

"Your father is a frightening man."

"He is a tyrant but he will pay for your suffering, yes? I am only one man and I am not violent but I will find a way to make him pay. He rules by violence and he might just die by violence."

Cateline's face paled. "But he is your father."

"An accident of birth, I assure you. My father has no love or pity in his heart and he will receive none from me."

Eric shivered at Larkin's vehemence and patted his sister's hand. "I am just glad we have you back, safe. Are you sure you're unhurt?"

"I'm fine, please don't worry. I honestly don't remember a lot of what happened."

**************

At dinner that night, Eric watched Gnohog carve roast venison and serve the Crown Prince of Serasya.

When they each had a plate before them, Ryall spoke. "Your Highness, you must stay here until we plan our next move. Our location is unknown to all except the inhabitants of Dorcliff."

"I will certainly appreciate it if Cateline can stay, but I cannot sit idle while Randolf holds Raulin prisoner. Onfroi and his obtuse son, Aldus, are a danger to all of

160

Oldegoth—not because they are clever, rather they have destabilized the kingdom. I need to…"

Larkin's voice faded, Eric's ears buzzed and the room went black. Somebody sobbed in the freezing dark and reached out to him. Pain and terror shook their every muscle and seeped across the void to Eric's mind.

"Where is Eric Man-Dragon?" The voice cut like jagged ice, the figure in the dark whimpered.

"I don't know—please—we weren't told—"

Eric knew that voice.

"Elite guardsman, Haman said he was sent on a mission but he didn't return, where is he?"

"I don't know—I wasn't told. Where is Haman?"

"Haman is my prisoner. He will be infused and become Wrygon-norce—or perhaps he'll die. Now tell me—where is the Man-Dragon?"

"I don't know! Please, let me go!"

"Oh no, I have chosen you and Eric Man-dragon to join my inner circle."

"No!"

A squeak of cork on glass and a pop. Eric saw a claw-like hand unstop a vial and a brittle fingernail dipped into the yellow liquid.

"You are little use to Lord Thornfingers as you are, let's see if I can change you into something he can use—"

A scream rent the blackness and Eric's eyesight cleared, a drop of sweat slid down his temple. The pain disappeared but his body trembled—somewhere in the night, the horror continued.

*Clarice?*

He inhaled and glanced around the table, none of his companions had shared the vision. Ryall debated Larkin over his need to seize the throne of Serasya.

"I respectfully suggest, your Highness, that you owe it to the people of Serasya to seize control of the Kingdom—if you don't, we'll see war and even worse, we may well see Inigo Thornfingers let loose, if as you say your father has people out searching for the Golden Hall."

Larkin set his fork down and took a sip of wine. "I fear you are right, they could stumble on it any day, yes? They have an idea of its location. I'm not convinced they'll find anything more than a skeleton—but who knows? He was a wizard; he could well have survived."

"Then you must act."

"I'm in dire need of an army, yes?" Larkin smiled. "There isn't many available to Dragon Ace, Larkin."

"Come with me, first thing in the morning. We'll talk to King Gnogoly of the Gigags."

"Do you think he will want to be involved?"

"I'm confident he'll help. He may want something in return of course, but the Gigags are not unreasonable. Bring Cateline—if you don't mind, Cateline." Ryall smiled at Cateline. "Old King Golly has a soft spot for pretty girls and you might give us some valuable leverage. Don't worry, he won't harm you."

Eric forced himself to eat, his appetite had disappeared but if Cateline saw him leave food on his plate, she would assume him sick. His heart thumped and waves of nausea washed over him as he saw over and over—the claw-like hand and the vial of yellow liquid.

**************

Eric went to bed that night and worried. Who was the tormentor? Who was the one tormented? He tried to concentrate; the voice was female. Clarice—he didn't want to accept it, in his heart he knew he saw Clarice. Mortal danger surrounded her.

Despair tightened Eric's throat, what had that man done to her? Did he go to Ryall and tell him what he saw? Ryall and Larkin had a monumental task ahead of them, securing the Gigag's allegiance. He could not distract them—if it might prevent freeing the terrifying Inigo Thornfingers, then Eric could not get under their feet.

He threw the covers back and sprang from his bed, dressed and crept from his room, across the parlour into the Dragon Hall.

*'Eric, why are you up so late?'*

*'I have to return to King's Port, Azuria.'*

*'Do you wish for me to take you?'*

*'Thanks, but I think I'll take Isuthiel—please understand.'*

*'I understand, of course. Please take care, Eric.'*

Eric moved on to Isuthiel's stall.

*'Your friend is in trouble, Eric.'*

# 32

Isuthiel settled in the bailey where Eric had trained with the Elite Guard.

'*Go back to Dorcliff, Isuthiel. You could be in danger here. Keep your mind open, I'll scry you when I need you.*'

The dragon's wings wafted cold air over Eric and Isuthiel disappeared into the night. Eric's heart raced as he moved through the ground level of the Tower of the Elite Guard, it stood open and deserted. He advanced and tried the door of The Keep—locked.

*Is the Galiron Crown safe?*

The door of the King's tower loomed ahead in the dark, worry and anger quickened his heartbeat. Eric's hands flew to his ears as throbbing pain bore in and forced his mind wide open. Voices spoke—his parents, his sister. Gilda and Raulin. Harsh laughter grated in his head. His face hit the cobblestones and the voices multiplied, men laughed, children cried and girls screamed. Sweat drenched him and blood pounded in his ears. Out of the darkness, a hand grasped his arm; something pricked his skin, his body stung with paralysing pain and oblivion fell.

"Don't fight them Eric, you're too precious. Just co-operate, the world of Eald D'Árian needs you."

Eric squinted against the blinding light, his head throbbed and his stomach heaved. Ropes bound him helpless. Men bore him along a dark corridor; Sir Cesper strode beside him, his face pale in the lamplight that flickered on the walls.

"Just go along with them, Eric. I'll talk to Randolf and get him to set you free. You'll have to be patient."

Down several flights of stairs, his captors dropped him on a cold damp floor, the ropes loosened and snaked away burning as they went. A scrape, a clang and footsteps faded. Silence and darkness swallowed him. Eric opened his eyes wide, trying to see; in his head, blinding lights flashed yellow and red. He retched; his stomach roiled, bile rose in his throat and sweat poured from his body. Somewhere above a door banged and echoed over the damp stone. Stench hung in the air, a sound of scratching came from somewhere close by.

"Hello?"

The scratching stopped at his voice. Eric held his breath and waited; the scratching resumed then an angry squeak.

*Rats.* He inhaled a ragged breath.

Hours later, the flashing lights in his vision cleared and his stomach settled; the cold sweats and shivers gradually eased. His throat hurt as he reached out for Clarice's spirit and found a lifeless void; his tears fell in the darkness. He searched for Raulin; he too looked upon a pitch-dark chamber. Eric pushed at the door of his King's mind, Raulin shoved him away but not before his weariness and sorrow touched Eric. He banged against the closed doors of Milo and Calder's minds.

*The people I need to scry are those who won't let me in.*

He cast his mind about for a friend and found Yrian, tossing and turning in troubled sleep. The knots and tangles of his friend's sleeping mind exhausted Eric, they told him of Yrian's plight; for four days, he'd had to work from first light until late into the night making weapons. His friend's new master strutted through the dream—Onfroi's son, Aldus. Yrian cowed, a strip of hard leather lashed and Aldus's cruel remarks cut deep. Eric couldn't hear the words but Yrian's pain and humiliation pierced Eric's soul and stirred a hell-fire of fury; the anger broke the connection to his friend's mind.

*At least I know he is still alive—albeit very unhappy.*

# 33

"Ryall, have you seen Eric?" Aalys entered the parlour where Ryall poked life and logs into the fire.

"Is he not in his room?"

"No."

"Check the dragon hall. He may have taken his dragons for a flight."

Eric's morning routine usually involved taking his dragons flying.

Ryall watched Aalys pad barefoot out the door and turned to poke his hand into the flames; satisfied the fire burned sufficiently hot he strode after Aalys.

"Why?" Aalys questioned the dragons aloud.

*'He said his friend, Clarice, was in danger—he told me to return to Dorcliff and he would summon me when he was ready.'* Isuthiel's talons squeaked on the flagstones, his tongue flicked. Tenebrozi chuffed clouds of black smoke.

Azuria's soft blue eyelids batted. *'He seemed distressed.'*

"We better go and find him."

"Aalys, how do you propose we find him? If he has been taken prisoner, any attempt on our part to rescue him might result in his death."

"Do you think he's alive?"

Ryall closed his eyes on his surroundings and lowered himself into Eric's mind. He shook him awake.

*'You and I are going to have a long talk, Eric Man-Dragon. Or should I say, Boy-Dragon?'*

*'Ryall, I'm sorry—my fellow guard, Clarice was being attacked—I thought I could get her out of here, but they caught me—I—'*

*'Where are you?'*

*'In the dungeons of Castle Greycliff, I think. Sir Cesper said he would try to get me released.'*

*'Sir Cesper? Who is he?'*

*'He's a knight, loyal to Raulin—a friend.'* A picture of Sir Cesper floated before Ryall.

*'Eric, what I need you to do is close your mind—even against me. Keep calm—don't allow yourself to become angry or distressed. Can you do that? If you don't you're leaving yourself open to attack.'*

*'I can try—'*

The younger Raigon-talth flung Ryall from his mind.

"Well, I guess he knows how to close me out at least."

"What are we going to do?"

"We need to talk to Prince Larkyn."

"He told us to call him Larkin."

"Yes, but somehow I can't."

"Me either."

*************

Ryall relaxed and eased into the Randolf's mind, the usurper King swayed in the Parlour of Castle Greycliff; the room shimmered with alcohol fumes. A shaft of pale sunlight slanted in the window.

Onfroi leaned in. "Put that bottle down and listen!"

Randolf's wine-soaked lip curled as he thumped the bottle on the table. "You dare order me around! I could have your head—"

"And I can withdraw my support and invite your brother back."

"Go ahead and try! He'll have your thick head off your shoulders in a heartbeat—bring him back, I challenge you!"

Randolf's wine-sodden gaze fixed on Onfroi; Aldus fidgeted beside his father, his eyes on the floor.

"You'll have to do something—challenging me isn't going to help your present circumstance."

"Maybe I don't care, Lord Onfroi—oh but that's right, I haven't granted you a lordship yet."

"What are you going to do about the servants?"

"What I'm going to do is tell you, and that—" Randolf's finger speared the air in front of Aldus's face. "—is go home and let me run the Kingdom! Because that idiot you call your son, is not going to treat my staff like slaves! Now get out and let me do my job!"

"I have more than one son, Randolf."

"That doesn't surprise me in the slightest."

"I feel the time has come to tell you who your father is."

"My father is—was—King Eustace."

A smirk twisted Onfroi's mouth. "Wrong. I am your father, Randolf."

Aldus's mouth fell open and he blinked stupidly. "Wa—"

"Rubbish!"

"Take a look in the mirror, Randolf, then look at Raulin. There is little family resemblance; why else would I want you elevated to King."

"Get out!"

"Think it over, my son—"

"Out!" Randolf's voice cracked, spit flew from his mouth and his red face purpled. "Get out of my parlour! Get out of my castle!"

Onfroi and Aldus scurried before his rage. The usurper King staggered and tipped the last dregs of wine into his mouth and muttered to himself.

"Father—rubbish! I'll not believe it!" He flopped into his chair and rang the bell. "That's right—no servants. My brother afforded his servants too much kindness, the first sign of tyranny they all walked out. Now I'm stuck here with Raulin's knights and Nutley."

A knock on the door snapped Randolf's last frayed nerve and the words, "What do you want now?" ripped from his throat.

"You Majesty?" Sir Cesper stepped in the door, his amber eyes moved from Randolf's to the bottle and back. "Can I have a word?"

"You can, but don't expect much in return. Aldus has caused my servants to leave—*en masse.*"

"Yes, I'm sorry. I will do whatever I can to encourage them to return. My knights and I will always remain loyal to Oldegoth."

"Oldegoth." Randolf hissed. "What was that word you wanted?"

"Last night, the guards imprisoned Eric of the Elite Guard—"

"Yes, snotty-nosed little mongrel, he sneaked in under the cover of darkness and earned himself a room in the dungeon."

"Perhaps it might be wise to at least assign him to guard duty, I'd be happy to keep an eye on him; he is little more than a boy."

Randolf belched and straightened. "I shall consider your proposal in seclusion, Sir Cesper; in the meantime he can stay where he is. Maybe I'll have his head off his shoulders if the mood should take me."

"Please, your Majesty, he will make a valuable guard—"

"I said I'd seclude it in cossession—success—just get out!"

Ryall chuckled, pulled himself out of Randolf's intoxicated mind and shook his head clear.

"Seems life is getting on top of the new King Randolf, he is not a happy man."

"It pleases me to hear this, yes?" Larkin smiled and forked a piece of fried egg into his mouth.

Ryall sipped his scalding tea. "Who is Sir Cesper?"

"He's the head of Raulin's knights, I'm not well acquainted with him but he is liked. In fact I've never heard a bad word about him."

"He was trying to get Randolf to release Eric. Not with any success though."

Cateline laid her fork down, her face pale. Larkin's arm curled around her shoulders.

"Let me see if I can see into Sir Cesper's mind." Ryall searched around and found Oldegoth's highest knight. As soon as he pushed into his mind, Ryall withdrew. He tried to shake away the sharp pain in his head.

"What happened?" Aalys peered into his face. "Did he kick you out?"

"No, I got in. I've just never experienced a mind like that—it hurt my head to be there." Ryall massaged his temples. He exhaled and addressed the Prince. "Is there one person in that castle that you can trust—someone who knows you?"

"There is only Nutley. He is quite disturbed in the mind but if I could talk to him, I'm sure he would help us. In fact, now that I think about it, with Reeve Calder gone from the castle, Nutley is the only person who can help us. There are many secret tunnels and hatches; Calder and Nutley know them all."

"Before we pay King Gnogoly a visit, let me try to contact Nutley. I'll need you to show him to me—you'll have to open your mind to me and let me see him."

Larkin tipped the last of his tea down his throat and got to his feet.

"Let us begin, shall we?"

Seated by the fire with Larkin and Cateline, Ryall relaxed and eased into the mind of his future King. A bent figure dressed in a rough spun cloak leaned on a hickory staff. Ryall familiarised himself with Nutley then withdrew from Larkin's mind.

"Is there something about Nutley that only you would know? Or anything—he may not believe that I'm acting for you when I communicate with him. I have to get him to trust me."

"Nutley is the name Raulin gave him. He has another name, which I cannot reveal—not without Raulin's permission—it begins with the letter H."

"If he is of unsound mind as you say, I may not be able to communicate with him. He's probably never had someone scry him before."

"I can assure you, Nutley will know what is going on."

Ryall opened and closed his mouth; he suppressed his curiosity about this person called Nutley.

"Very well. Let me try." Ryall's mind zoomed away to Castle Greycliff.

# 34

A flurry of brooms, mops, brushes, rakes, and shears, cleaned and trimmed Port Mortlock, the capital of L'Áscarle; a royal decree set every able-bodied man, woman, and child to work. The imminent arrival of the Crown Prince of Serasya galvanised the Gigags to action. It would never do for the Prince to think the Gigags slothful.

The Gigag King Gnogoly the Robust had the royal court in an uproar.

"Did you find my sceptre, Gnokol?"

"I have the servants searching your Majesty, to no avail."

"I don't care if you have to turn the palace kee-kaw, find it!" King Gnogoly waved his big hands about him. "What is this Prince famous for? I believe he fled his father fourteen years ago. Has he invented anything or composed an air? Or poetry? Has he written an opus?"

"Sire, I believe he is a Dragon Ace."

"A Dragon Ace!" Inspiration ignited in King Gnogoly's eyes. "Indeed!"

"He rides dragons for sport; I'm told he is one of the best."

"Excellent! A greater achievement than those of his father King Guidion di Dyum the Picaroon. Filching around hunting for their so-called Golden Hall—brangling and breedbating—"

"I believe they have located it, Sire."

"Hah! They can graff and grub all they want—what do they expect to find?"

"Their saviour, Lord Inigo Thornfingers, Sire."

"A thousand years, wasting away in a mined-out cavern, trapped underground—"

Gnokol picked up his King's thread. "If he survived the initial avalanche and then one thousand years of hibernation, it's unlikely he will have vitality sufficient to wage war, Sire. No, it's his disciples we must fear, your Majesty, therein lies true evil."

"How thou speaketh, Preceptor Gnokol? The truth? I fear you do. But quickly, I need my sceptre! Do you think the Prince will carry his?"

"I speak the truth, Your majesty, when I venture he most likely doesn't own one."

Gnogoly pivoted to gape at his Preceptor. "Do you think so?"

"He fled his father at age twelve and has since led the life of a commoner."

A bark of Gigag laughter thundered in the parlour. "Then leave my sceptre where it is! A true king has no need for such a trivial object."

**************

At midday, the bells of Port Mortlock began ringing and King Gnogoly inhaled a half pint of ale. Preceptor Gnokol thumped his back.

"Quickly, Reelpot Gnobung! Come—bring the King more blashy!"

"Nay—nay, bid my valet to fetch me a clean blouse and snotterclout, hurry!" King Gnogoly boomed another cough.

Watery-eyed and spluttering but sporting a clean blouse and handkerchief, the King hurried to join his consort, Gnigilly and fellow aristocrats on the dais in the city square. The clamour of bells continued as the city folk gathered to welcome an important visitor.

"Prythee! Whence doth he loom?"

"From yonder—"

"Behold! Dragons!"

"Wherefore?"

"Nay, squint-a-pipes, ye wink-a-peeps behold birdies in the nyle!"

"Naught, thou lickspigot! How thou blutters! Behold—"

"Hush thine whoopub!"

"Yarken! His Nibs, Crown Prince of Serasya looms!"

The citizens of Port Mortlock fell silent as three dragons winged towards them. A big green beast glided above the street, a common red on either side.

"Welcome, Crown Prince, Guidion di Larkyn, welcome!" King Gnogoly and the Gigags bowed low. "Welcome Raigon-talth, Ryall and Aalys! Welcome, my friends, to Port Mortlock!"

**************

King Gnogoly and his consort, Gnigilly, hosted an alfresco luncheon with gnome jousting, poetry, music, and dance for his guest's entertainment. Larkin and his party reclined on an elevated lawn bordered by a rose garden. White furniture, fine linen cloths, bone china, crystal jugs and silver trays of delicacies surrounded them. White uniformed servants waited on their every whim.

At mid-afternoon, King Gnogoly showed his guests to their rooms.

"Please, make yourselves at home. You have servants at your disposal, anything you need, ring the bell. The feast will begin at sunset."

**************

"I cannot eat another crumb." Cateline's voice reached Larkin over the hubbub and clatter of guests around the King's table.

"Yes, no more crug and clotterpot for me either." Larkin smiled and sipped some water. The Gigag King's table had sagged under the feast, a table that stretched the length of the hall with Gigag aristocrats elbow to elbow along each side. Like the King, they spoke fluent D'Árian but as the evening wore on, occasional outbreaks of Gigaggian reached Larkin's ears.

"Would'st thou like a clean plate, your Royal Highness?" A servant appeared at his elbow. "A fresh muckender? Some fresh cutlery?"

"No, thank you. I am afraid I have already glopped too—er—over-indulged."

"Shall I bod the reel-pot to bring thee some more blashy or wine?"

"Thank you, yes—blashy."

"You're learning." Cateline murmured in his ear.

**************

177

The aristocrats had bid them goodnight and Larkin, Cateline, Ryall, and Aalys, at last had King Gnogoly's substantial ear.

"So you see, your Majesty," Larkin worried he may have froth at the corner of his mouth after a long pitch to the Gigag King, "I fear the only solution for the Kingdom of Serasya is I depose my father, no? It is only a matter of time and he will open the Golden Hall and if the legend of Thornfingers proves true, Eald D'Árian may descend into chaos."

"Thornfingers!" King Gnogoly snorted. "Indeed! You are very young, Prince."

Larkin waited for Gnogoly to continue.

"Yes—I fear. Young and possibly unwise."

Larkin's eyes met Ryall's and the elder Raigon-talth winked.

"Wisdom comes with age." Gnogoly tipped a generous portion of wine down his throat; it cascaded noisily over his tonsils, gurgled past his larynx and splashed over his dinner in exchange for a royal ructus. "But we have no time to wait for age begotten wisdom so we must avail ourselves of the next option."

Larkin's mouth opened and closed. Some answers arrived without a question. He waited.

"Yes. I have a solution. Yes—you will have my allegiance on one condition." The King raised a sturdy finger. "Marriage."

Larkin quailed. "But—"

"You have the perfect wife seated beside you."

"Oh. Yes." Larkin exhaled in relief—he had feared a Gigag princess waited in the wings. "She is perfect, is she not?"

"She is! She is! And you must marry her."

"I must? Well yes—"

"Why not—why wait? Go on, propose! Take all the space you need!" Gnogoly's big hand gestured around him.

Larkin shrugged and grinned. He rose, pulled Cateline to her feet and knelt before her. "Cateline, will you do me the honour of becoming my wife?"

Cateline blushed cherry-red; she laughed and nodded. "Yes."

King Gnogoly interrupted the applause from Ryall and Aalys; disappointment clouded his brown eyes.

"We Gigags propose differently to you D'Árians. Our females demand we demonstrate our prowess; we must sing, recite, dance or perform acrobatics. One young man in my youth invented an iron contraption on wheels, powered by fire and water to present to his intended." The King's laughter bounced off the walls and the arm of his chair shook under a hefty smack. "Called it a steam horse! Utter nonsense, but she married him anyway." Gnogoly pause to wipe a mirthful tear. "But I ramble! We have not time now to teach you the subtleties of romance. So, three days hence, I shall preside over your nuptials and hand-banding."

"Does this mean the Prince has your allegiance?" Ryall brought the meeting back to a more serious subject.

"Certainly! Certainly! The Gigags love peace but sometimes for peace to endure, war must be waged and if it be necessary, it would honour us to lend our swords to the King in Waiting."

Larkin dragged his eyes away from his beautiful fiancée. "I thank you, your Majesty. Without your support, my position would be untenable."

"Let us enjoy your nuptials and then I will gather my Dragon Knights to accompany us to Asyann."

**************

"The Gigags have forged these rings of the finest gold, a gift from the Isle of L'Áscarle to the Kingdom of Serasya. Long may our people live in harmony…" King Gnogoly couldn't keep the smile off his face, nor the tears from his eyes as he presided over the marriage of the Crown Prince of Serasya to the commoner, Cateline of Oldegoth. The Gigags loved a rags-to-riches romance. Happy sniffles issued from the around the cathedral as the Gigags mopped their eyes with sodden snotterclouts.

"…and so by the power passed to me by my forefather's and upheld by my people's grace, I pronounce thee man and wife. May no force—be it nature, D'Árian, Gigag, Slokk, or Dragon put asunder what we today have blessed. The bride must now toss her tuzzy-muzzy and you, Prince Larkyn, may kiss your wife."

To the thunder of Gigags stamping feet and clapping hands, Larkin kissed his bride. The powerful voice of a Gigag woman sang the recessional and the celebrations moved on to the palace lawn for yet another feast.

# 35

From the deep sand of his stall, Isuthiel jerked awake. The screams of his dream continued in his waking mind.

*'Do you hear it too, Isuthiel?'* Azuria ambled across the flagstones to the open doors.

*'Dragons! They're under attack, we must help.'* Tenebrozi's scales rustled as he shook off the sand.

Aggression rumbled in Isuthiel's breast, his talons gouged the flagstones as he stretched, flexed, and primed his sinuous body for combat. Tenebrozi and Azuria slunk through the doors, their tails twitched and tongues flicked. Bolder than his nest mates, Isuthiel flung himself from the cliff-edge into the morning sky, he searched for the disturbance and found it; far below on a wide sandy beach, Emperor Gernellian attacked a group of dragons. With wings hugged to his body, Isuthiel rocketed downwards, Tenebrozi followed.

*'Stay behind, Azuria—you're not a warrior.'*

*'That does not mean I'm defenceless.'*

A blaze of common reds flew in the opposite direction to Isuthiel, their screams rebounded off the cliffs.

As the Golden Wyvern loomed below him, fear nudged aside Isuthiel's anger. Emperor Gernellian dwarfed the young dragons, seven times over; the lack of fire and front talons did not hinder his attack on the docile Common Dragons—a dozen of them lay on the beach, suffocating and burning from acidic wyvern spittle.

Isuthiel hit the wyvern's back, talons ripped the golden hide, and scales tore free. Gernellian's enormous head twisted as Isuthiel fanged his neck. Stinging acid filled Isuthiel's mouth, he roared green and white flames, searing the yellow hide; the wyvern's neck flexed and flung the dragon away. Isuthiel plunged into the raging surf and swallowed mouthfuls of salt water, his head snaked beneath the waves. He came up for air, regurgitated water and wyvern acid—nausea flooded from head to tail, to the tips of his wings. The world spun as he looked back to see a Tenebrozi-sized hole rip in Gernellian's wing membrane as the black dragon hit it at speed, a crack split the air and the wyvern screamed.

*'Through his wing like flying through hoops.'* He dipped, skimmed the sand and splashed into the waves. *'What did you think of my flying, Isuthiel?'*

*'Isuthiel!'* Azuria landed beside her nest mates. *'Biting the neck of a wyvern would normally get you killed. As luck would have it—he'd depleted his acid stores attacking the others.'*

*"The taste alone is enough to kill. I feel—so—"*

Roaring and spitting from the crimson ducts under his tongue, Gernellian dragged his broken wing across the beach, the acid sack behind his jaw gaped open, blood and yellow fluid dripped onto the sand.

*'Quickly Isuthiel! Fly.'*

Panic pulled him skyward—his courage dissolved. Up the cliff face he flew. Isuthiel's anger and shame burned more than Gernellian's acid—he should have known he and Tenebrozi could not defeat the gigantic wyvern unassisted.

*'Where is Azuria?'* Wide eyed with fear, Tenebrozi greeted him in front of the Dragon Hall.

**************

Azuria lowered contrite eyes to the sand; her wings folded to her sides. She waited; the wyvern drew near and stopped.

*'I beg your permission to speak, Your Royal Highness, Almighty.'*

*'Speak, Dragon.'*

*'Your Majesty, please allow me to help you.'*

*'Help? I should kill you, blue female—you condemn yourself by association.'*

*'Please, your magnificence, allow me to assist. I am a healer."*

*'A healer? There are no healers left on Dorcliff.'*

*'I'm only a lowly common dragon from Oldegoth, your Majesty, but I can heal your injuries.'*

**************

*'Your sister is a traitor!"* A red Common Dragon skidded to a halt before Isuthiel, his words arrived on chuffs of black smoke. *'She tends the tyrant, Gernellian, so he can attack us again!'*

*'I trust my sister!'*

*'I do too!'* Tenebrozi shuffled and his tongue flicked across his lips, black smoke puffed from his nose.

More Common Dragons settled beside the red, their chests glowed orange and yellow; their talons scored the flagstones of the dragon hall forecourt.

Isuthiel arched his neck and bared his fangs. *'If any of you approach my sister you will answer to me!'* He didn't betray his heart-load of doubts. For five days, Azuria had tended Gernellian. He and Tenebrozi watched from afar as their sister flew back and forth, gathering medicines from all over the island. She slept on the beach within hailing distance of Gernellian. They dare not approach her, fearing Gernellian would kill her if it appeared her loyalty to him wavered. Isuthiel tried to scry Eric, but Ryall had ordered him to close his mind and Eric had done just that. He hoped Ryall would return soon for Isuthiel worried. Azuria too, had closed her mind.

*Does Gernellian have her under a spell? Has she lost her mind and switched loyalties? Or is she sabotaging him?*

Isuthiel chose to believe the latter, the other scenarios didn't bear thinking about.

**************

*'Your Majesty, are your talons paining you?'* Azuria dropped her gaze to the sand.

*'They always pain me, Female, ever since I moved to this damp and decaying island. It vexes my tail as well.'*

*'It is a fungus that afflicts Your Magnificence and as always, you're right when you say the damp causes it. I would be honoured to apply poultices for five days; they will ease your discomfit.'*

*"Do it. And bring me more of those magma lozenges.'*

*'Are they helping with the pain, your Majesty?'*

*'They are.'*

*'It grieves me greatly, your Royal Radiance, to advise you to keep your magnificent wing still. Even the strongest and most powerful bones take time to mend. Please—allow me to warm the sand for your Majesty.'* Azuria puffed flames, warming and stirring until a wyvern sized patch radiated heat. *'If it pleases Your Magnificence, I will now hasten to gather more medicines to comfort your distress.'*

*'See to it.'* The enormous wyvern grunted and huddled in the warm sand.

Away to the other side of the island, Azuria gathered her ingredients. Gibbsite crystals from the mountainside. Down to the salt-flats for nahcolite. Up on the cliff she gathered soft white kaolin. To the Raigon-talth's garden for cloves of garlic and roots of horseradish. On a shallow basin in a rock, shaped over thousands of years by healers gone before her, she milled them and mixed them, adding her saliva for moisture. She divided the sticky mixture into balls and rolled them in powdered willow bark. From a seep in the mountainside, she scraped together moss and piled it high. Azuria held a treasure of information deep in her brain—inherent knowledge, heritage for her life's vocation.

# 36

Prince Guidyon di Elyot brooded at the open window; mist rolled in and rimed on his facial stubble. His heart hurt; his father had killed Cateline. He cursed his brother for failing to rescue her—did she mean so little to him? They threw her from the cliffs of Dionysia, even if she had landed in deep water and by some miracle, survived the fall—the freezing sea would have claimed her life in seconds.

*'Tis foolish of you to even dream such a lovely woman would spare you a passing glance.*

Fate of birth cursed Prince Guidyon di Elyot to the meanest life of a cripple—only his highborn status prevented the cruel gibes he saw on the lips of peasants as he scrabbled past on mismatched legs, his left arm curled against his torso. Even when he stood straight on his good leg, he wasn't tall like his older brother, Prince Guidyon di Larkyn. He hadn't seen his brother for fourteen years but didn't doubt he had grown into a handsome man.

An end to his reverie announced itself with a knock on the door.

"Enter." A rivulet of icy water slid down his face and hung from the tip of his nose.

A click, a clunk, and a squeak—the door swung inward; the King's seneschal entered, flanked by guards. The man cast a frigid glance at the open window.

"The King has commanded your presence in his private chamber, your Highness."

"Yes, could you give me a moment? I need to don suitable attire."

"Very well, your Highness."

Elyot put on his finest raiment and feather-bedecked *chapeau.* He joined the men waiting at the door.

"Take me to my King."

Elyot limped in their wake, down the stairs of the prince's tower and along the passage to the King's tower. The King's personal guard planted himself in their path and saluted.

"Even his Royal Highness, Prince Guidyon di Elyot must not enter the King's chamber so armed."

Elyot permitted the removal of his sword and dagger.

"I will secure them until your meeting with the King is done." The seneschal rolled the sword belt around the weapon and bowed.

"This way, if it pleases you, your Highness." The guard held the door wide and Elyot hobbled in. "Please, take a seat. The King shall receive you presently."

Alone in his father's parlour, Elyot withdrew a tiny vial and a handkerchief from his jacket.

*Evil shall be answered with evil, father of mine.*

The cork came away easily and stinging drops of gaseous liquid dropped onto the kerchief.

*An eye for an eye, Father Dearest.*

"Well, Prince Elyot," King Guidyon di Dyum's sudden appearance sent a frisson juddering down Elyot's twisted spine. His father revealed a rare, buoyant mood.

"You will be pleased to know, my scouts have located the Golden Hall of Serasya. The Gigags secret is no more. Lord Thornfingers will emerge from his prison and punish his enemies."

"I've told you father, Lord Thornfingers never punishes—he only forgives and blesses."

"Nonsense!" The King turned to the sideboard and chose a heavy-based bottle. "Come—drink with me, son, for victory is only days away and our hegemony will follow. I have sent forty of my best men to Oldegoth to capture your brother. Lord Onfroi of King's Port has sworn his allegiance—little good that will do him when we invade…"

As his father spoke, Elyot approached from behind, reached over his shoulder and clasped a linen kerchief, laced with oblivion, to the cruel mouth. The King's eyes bulged and glazed as the sting of ether pervaded his airways. Elyot eased his father to the floor and drew a long, silver hatpin from among the feathers of his chapeau. He paused to knot a length of fine thread around the jewelled crook—the purpose-built head of a purpose-built pin. Up the nose of his unconscious father, with the heel of his hand, Elyot hammered the pin into the cruel brain of his father, deeper he pushed; his little finger buried to the second knuckle. He wriggled the pin and withdrew it by the fine thread. Blood poured from the King's nose. Elyot wiped the pin clean, cast the linen kerchief into the hearth, and flung the tiny vial from the window to a rooftop below. His trembling fingers groped the King's throat in search of a heartbeat. Guidyon di Dyum's pulse fluttered like an injured bird and faded to naught. Elyot admired the jewelled crook of the hatpin as he secreted it among the feathers and returned the chapeau to his head.

"Help!" He flung the door wide and wailed into the corridor. "Help! My father has collapsed—help!"

# 37

A sound in the gloom had penetrated his fevered sleep and jolted Eric awake. Someone leaned over him.

The voice wheezed and rattled. "Come, Master Eric."

"What!" Eric sat up, his sleep fuddled eyes adjusted too slow in the darkness. "Who are you?" The hair on the back of Eric's neck prickled; nobody came down here in the middle of the night.

"Shhh! Make no sound. Now come, follow—I'm going to free you."

"I want to know who you are before I follow you."

"It's I, Nutley at your service, Master Eric. I'm here to help."

"Nutley! Are you feeling well?"

"Nutley is never well, Master. Nutley just is."

"What are you going to do to me? I might be safer to stay where I am." Nutley had shown little compassion in the past and Eric's years on the streets taught him caution.

"Master Larkin has ordered your release. You must come—even a Raigon-talth will die here in the deepest deep."

"Larkin? That's different then. Lead the way, Nutley."

On his feet, Eric moved towards the iron bars that had held him captive.

"Not that way!" Nutley hissed, he grasped the hem of Eric's tunic and led him to the corner. "In here! Quickly! Take care—"

The hickory staff nudged Eric forward and he almost fell down a hole in the floor. His feet found a slippery stone stairs with no handrails. Eric's Raigon-talth eyes penetrated the pitch dark; he kept one hand on the wall knowing it wouldn't save him if he slipped. From behind him came the soft clunk of stone on mossy stone as Nutley closed the trapdoor.

At last, he found a level cobble stone floor; he stopped to get his bearings.

"Come Master Eric," Nutley's cold hand took his arm; his claw like nails prickled Eric's skin. "This way." Nutley unblocked his throat and coughed. "You smell like Nutley," he rudely observed.

"Like unwashed leggings with a dead rat stuffed inside?"

"No—no!" Nutley snorted back his nasal drip, "No, you smell really bad!"

"Has Randolf granted me a pardon?"

"No."

"Well, why are you releasing me—how—?"

"I told you, I am obeying Master Larkin's orders.

"But Larkin is—um—away." Eric stopped himself revealing Larkin's whereabouts. "Where is Randolf?"

"Sleeping."

"Aren't you afraid he'll wake and catch you? One of his servants might—"

"He has no servants, they all walked out, said they'd rather starve than work for Onfroi and his son."

"What if Onfroi catches you."

"Randolf has barred him entry into the castle—he has closed the drawbridge." Nutley led Eric across a narrow stone bridge, far below a stream gushed and bubbled. Their voices and footsteps echoed in the cavernous space.

"Why?"

"The truth can be a painful thing and some have little tolerance for pain. Randolf became very distressed and drank every last drop of wine in the castle, then he searched for something more to ease his anguish."

"Did he find it?"

Nutley wheezed, sniffed, coughed and spat. "He did, or rather, I did and I left it where he could find it."

Eric stopped. "What did you give him?"

"Laudanum, Master Eric." Nutley tugged on Eric's tunic, urging him on.

"What's laudanum?"

"Something to ease the burden of a tormented mind."

"Well, that's very kind of you, Nutley."

"Not kind, Master Eric. Not kind at all. A healthy mind is one that faces its demons head-on. Yes, head-on. Tis different when treating physical injuries—terrible injuries—yes." A clunk echoed in the dark and Nutley opened a heavy door. "This way, Master Eric. Mind the stairs."

Torches lit the way as Nutley led Eric up a series of stairs to a door Eric recognised.

"This is Larkin's house."

"It is, Master Eric, it is."

"Is Milo home?"

"Milo is in hiding, Master Eric, with the other Wizards. Onfroi has ordered their deaths—the reward is a purse of silver. Basil and the men of the City Watch are searching high and low. Wise men can hide in plain sight when mundane eyes seek. Come I will pour you a bath."

"A bath would be most welcome."

Nutley filled the bath with steaming water and placed a clean flannel on the chair.

"Give me your clothes, I will launder them."

"Thank you, Nutley."

Eric lay back in the warm water and imagined travelling back to a time where riding his dragons in the Coliseum presented his greatest challenge. If Isuthiel hadn't scratched him would he still be here today, facing a war he never dreamed would come? Onfroi would still have seized control of the Kingdom but what difference would it have made to a budding dragon ace? His mind journeyed the well-worn path to Clarice, he scried the void and found darkness. He examined the red spot of tethered skin on his inner arm. What had pierced it as Onfroi's men carried him to the dungeon? He recalled the searing pain and nausea when they had left him in that foul darkness—a similar illness to that he'd suffered with Isuthiel's first scratch.

Nutley returned with more warm water.

"Nutley, has the new King changed life for the people of the city?"

"Drastically, Master Eric."

"In what way?"

"Many merchants have closed their doors. Either because their supplies have been cut off or because they don't want to be seen co-operating with Onfroi. His treasonous behaviour has stalled the city of King's Port. Ships are diverting to Esterhaven rather than risk having their cargo seized to feed Onfroi's troops and prolong the siege. Farmers risk arrest as they slip away in the night to take their produce to other markets. The people of King's Port will surely starve if Randolf remains in power."

# 38

Clean once more, Eric had a meal of Nutley's soup, not the finest but better than the odd dish of gruel someone had pushed through the bars in the dungeon.

"I must leave as soon as possible, Nutley. I need to return to Dorcliff and alert the other Raigon-talth."

"Yes, Master Eric. I fear Oldegoth faces its darkest hour, an enemy marches on us, an enemy much worse than Onfroi and his son."

Fear danced down Eric's spine. "Who are they?"

"Wrygon-norce, Master Eric. Venin born but the blood in their veins is sour and toxic. Not the sweet fire that flows in the veins of the Raigon-talth. Wrygon-norce occur when a person is spat on by a Wyvern hatchling. No, we must restore Raulin to the throne; he is the leader Oldegoth needs."

"Where is Raulin?"

"He is shut in The Keep. I can feed him but cannot speak to him. I know many secret tunnels in this castle but even I cannot free him from there, Randolf took the key from me and keeps it hidden."

"Nutley, how did Gilda die?"

"She died with honour, defending her King."

"Who killed her?"

"Tomas."

"Tomas? But Tomas was of the Elite Guard—why would he turn on his own?"

"I know not, Master Eric. Gilda killed him before he could reveal his other master, though I think 'tis certain he served Onfroi."

Eric finished his meal in silence, trying to fathom what malice or promises might have motivated Tomas to such treachery. A splutter from Nutley drew his attention.

"Before you leave, Master Eric, I must make a confession. Who better to confess to than the third Raigon-talth?"

"Nutley?"

Nutley's lower lip trembled and he burst into tears. "I have done something terrible! I have disgraced my order!"

"Order?"

"The Order of St Alúthien—my order; long had the ancient wizards abandoned it. It is my order; I revived it for I alone knew the prophecy. I knew the order had to be resurrected!" Larkin's kitchen echoed Nutley's sobs.

"You? But—"

"I am the seventh wizard, the head of The Order of St Alúthien!"

"The seventh wizard was, um—let me think— Hectar. He's interred under the King's tower."

*Is Nutley living some kind of fantasy?*

"That body in the tomb is not mine. He was a vagrant that died on the Castle Bridge. I am Hectar, though I am not worthy to call myself a wizard, I am not worthy to be part of The Order." His sobs subsided to hiccoughs.

Eric gaped, stunned.

*This means The Order of St Alúthien still has seven wizards.*

Nutley mopped his face with his cloak sleeve. "Yes, there are still seven wizards."

*Did you just read my thoughts?*

"What was it you needed to confess?"

"Randolf is only half a prince." Nutley gave a wet sniff, "He has a different sire. He is not the son of King Eustace."

"Really?"

*I wonder does Raulin know.*

"Yes, Raulin knows, it was the last thing the King told him."

It disturbed Eric that Nutley seemed to read his thoughts.

"Well, whose son is he?"

"He has bad blood. Queen Elena should never have allowed such evil to enter the King's bedchamber." Nutley's face flickered a warm yellow in light from the candle. "Onfroi is an evil man. He cuckolded the King then poisoned him. He was going to poison Prince Raulin too but I would give him no more. No more! He told me he wanted to kill rats—I believed him!" Nutley cracked himself across the temple with his staff, blood formed tiny beads on the welt. "It's all my fault! My fault! I knew of his treachery, I knew! Why didn't I know he would murder my King? If he'd commit high treason against the King's house, of course he would murder the King!" A wheezy wail escaped Nutley's mouth.

"So what—tell it to me again, from the start?" Eric needed to get it straight in his head.

"I knew the Queen was taking Onfroi to her bed. He was always in the King's tower when the King wasn't." Nutley's pale eyes glimmered in the dim light. "The King knew what she was doing but he loved her. She didn't deserve his love. She should never have taken such evil into the King's bed. She paid for it. Oh yes! She paid for her treachery when she died giving birth to that devil spawn! The good King raised that boy as one of his own. I would have cast him from the battlements!"

Nutley lowered his crooked frame into a chair. "But Onfroi wasn't content to have taken the King's honour. He wanted his son to be King. He came to me and asked for poison, said he had botheration with rats in his stables, many rats. So I sold him arsenic. His evil knows no bounds! He gave the powder to Prince Randolf with instructions to sprinkle it on the King's plate. That boy didn't know he was poisoning his King; the man he believed was his father! Onfroi intended to kill Prince Raulin in the same manner." Nutley's chest heaved and he gulped. "When I realized what was afoot I hastened to tell King Eustace. He was already gravely ill."

He paused to wipe the tears.

"I left the King's side to fetch what I knew to be an antidote, from my apothecary, but I was waylaid by Onfroi's men. They beat me; they kicked me until they thought I was dead—I thought I was dead! Then my King came for me. He carried me with the last of his strength back to his parlour. I lay dying beside my King. Eustace blessed Raulin and passed him the crown. He said to his son, 'your brother must never, never wear this crown. For the sake of Oldegoth and all we hold dear, he must never wear the crown.'

"Prince Raulin, Prince Larkyn, and Milo carried me to this house, they nursed me back to health and they gave me this name. They ordered me to stay in the confines of the castle, and never to reveal who I am. Only King Raulin the Redeemer and his closest friends know who Nutley really is. Until now. Now Eric man-dragon, the Venin Born knows."

"This means that the prophecy could still be true."

"The Prophecy. Yes! I believe it will prove very true. Hope, and a warning imparted by an ancient sage."

"But we still don't know—we can't read all of the scroll." Eric's excitement faded. "There's still pieces we don't know."

"We don't need the scroll, young master; I can tell you what the prophecy says. My grandmother passed it down to me. She learned it from her forefathers."

"You know it all? Please Nutley; we need to know all of it, and if it is important." *Or just a piece of nonsense.*

Nutley's voice gained strength as he recited: "When the dead bell tolls, seven wizards of olde, restore the order of Saint Alúthien. Dragons, four score and many more, and the Raigon-talth three shall gather for war. Of the venin born throng, the youngest is strong; he shall lead his confrere through the murk. Oldegoth must fight when the beacons ignite and restore innocence to Eald D'Árian once more."

Eric's scalp prickled.

*The youngest is strong. I'm the youngest, how am I strong?*

"Now, Master Eric. You should get a good night's sleep." Nutley pushed himself upright. "It may be days before you'll sleep again."

# 39

*I am Gralix the Whisperer. Shut in this mine for an age, my vitality has paled to the meanest existence, my life-force wanes in the darkness. It has been years since the light of my master's spirit flickered and died but ever do his bones cling to my shoulders, our existence eternally bound.*

*The evil Gyarie, Goddess of Serasya, stole the Galiron Crown from his head, robbing his heart of magic. Gyarie and her sorcery vanished from Eald D'Arian and forsook the people to impiety. The Gigag miners lured us with gilded promises and shut us into this depleted burrow.*

*Now a tremble in the abyss shakes my prison of stone and the voices of men ravage my ears. I feel but not see the stabs of light reflected in my blinded eyes. Freedom belated is liberty denied and their one reward shall be death.*

**************

A crash and rumble in the abyss shook the northern face of Dorcliff. The men who moved the rubble ran for their lives, out of the cavern and onto the ledge. They scattered as a giant pillar, eighty feet tall, toppled and thundered down the mountainside. Below, enormous waves rolled across the sea.

"Stay where you are!" Sir Grimilyn, the knight that King Guidion di Dyum sent to oversee the task, glared around him. "It's just a tremor, it will settle in a few moments!"

"Sir, something has been moving about in there for hours."

"We are trying to free a living being, Hadyn—it's a good thing that something is moving about."

"It might be Tagrali himself—"

"Don't be stupid, Tagrali is a myth." Getyner, a dour faced man scowled at Hadyn. "So is Inigo Thornfingers. All stupid faddoodle made up to scare little kids—and some stupid adults."

"No! You're wrong—"

"The tremor has stopped now all of you get back to work!"

Through the morning, uninterrupted by further tremors, the men worked. Sweat and toil shrank the rubble at the entrance to the cavern; at last, they made an opening large enough for a man to crawl through.

"Is there one among you brave enough to take a look inside?" Sir Grimilyn stared down his nose at the exhausted men. "Or are you all white-livered and slothful?"

Averted eyes and shuffling feet met Sir Grimilyn's request.

"Getyner, you're not a big man, you'll easily fit through that hole and you've told us you fear not what is inside. Take this torch and crawl up there; tell us what you see."

Getyner paled but took the torch. Stone by stone he climbed, sweat trickled down his face in spite of the cold mist floating in from the sea. Dislodged stones clattered from his scrabbling feet and rolled down to the men whose upturned eyes watched, wide and fearful. Hand over hand he gained the top, pushed into the opening and held the torch high.

"'It's a foul breath that looms from the deep." He coughed and the torch brightened in the sulphurous vapour and illuminated a thousand years of darkness and decay. Before him stood an enormous, translucent pink dragon, Gralix the Whisperer, on his back the skeleton of Inigo Thornfingers. Balls of white cloud quivered in Gralix's eye sockets; rotting skin draped over the skull that swayed on trembling neck. Gossamer strips of wing membranes, chewed by cave-weevils, hung on wasted bones, and brittle curls of overgrown talons tangled around its feet. White mist hissed from crumbling teeth; the monster expended its residual spirit to lunge and fall at Getyner's feet. The skeleton crashed to the floor, the skull bounced and came to rest inches from Getyner's face. He screamed at the empty sockets and grinning mouth and threw the torch into the cavern; the gas exploded and blew the men down the mountainside with the remains of Inigo Thornfingers and his dragon. Through the flying rubble, dust and flames flashed an apparition; the spectre of a tall man riding an enormous dragon sped away into the mist. The foundations of the mountain shook and the quake thundered around the Brimstone Archipelago. The line of volcanos came to life and spewed molten lava into the waves. To the east, the Rock of Wycliff—a six thousand foot monolith—roared and belched fire from fissures over its craggy surface. The wave-worn base cracked, the home of the Wyverns crumbled and toppled into the Parinith Strait, taking with it many of its inhabitants; the survivors took to the skies and sought refuge on the neighbouring islands. The sea heaved and tossed, gigantic waves rolled and crashed; the ship carrying Serasya's forty best fighting men sank into the murky depths.

**************

Eric stared, bemused. From his vantage point at the top of the Gate Tower, he watched a procession of children, hundreds ranging in age from around three years old to their mid-teens.

"What is it I'm seeing, Nutley?"

"I fear it is the future of King's Port—of Oldegoth, Master Eric."

Men in jute robes, some on horseback herded them into the City Square. Eric's anger soared as a boy of similar age to him broke from the line. A man fell him with a pole, hauled him to his feet and forced him to return, stumbling in the line.

"Who are those men with the poles?"

"They're the Monks of St Saxxa, Master Eric. From the Monastery."

"Where did all these children come from?"

"Some of them wear the hopsack of an orphan but many of them are children of Oldegoth—stolen from their parents is my guess, Master Eric."

"Stolen! Why are they being marched to the square?"

"Failed Wizard Tagrali needs many children if he is to subdue the people of Oldegoth. Tagrali's evil is infinite, Master Eric."

"But what is he going to use them for, they're just kids! And why are the monks taking his side? I thought they were a force for good."

"They lost their true purpose a long time ago. When the Lady Gyarie, Goddess of Serasya withdrew from the physical world, she left little for spiritual folk to embrace so they turned to the one who offered them leadership. It is my belief that the monks have supplied Tagrali with orphans for many years. Many children have disappeared from the orphanage; many mothers who'd had to surrender their illegitimate babies complained their children disappeared, usually at around ten years of age. The monks have always been able to show papers proving the children were adopted."

"What does Tagrali do with them?" Eric feared he knew the answer and braced himself.

"Yes, Eric—you know the answer. He infuses them with the acid of a Wyvern hatchling and turns them into Wrygon-norce. Less than one in four survives and they endure awful pain and infirmity, but I don't need to tell you, Master Eric, for I sense you well recall the pain when the dragon hatchling marked you."

"I—are you reading my mind, Nutley?"

"Reading no. Your thoughts are unguarded, Master Eric, they leak from your head like steam from the Rock of Wycliff."

"We have to do something about this, Nutley."

"Yes, you mustn't let the enemy read your thoughts."

"No, I mean this." Eric opened his hand to the scene below. "We must free Raulin—the King. We must rally the knights—"

Nutley hissed. "Knights!"

"Surely Sir Cesper can do something about this, we need to—"

"What I need you to do, Master Eric, is go back to Dorcliff and rally the Raigon-talth. I will also ask you to light the beacon, to call for aid from the provinces."

"Do you think they'll come?"

"It is my guess, Master Eric, that most of the King's subjects are yet to discover he has been deposed by his treasonous half-brother—Oldegoth is a large kingdom. When they see one beacon alight, they'll hasten to light theirs, and the next will do the same until they're all blazing."

"The beacon tower is heavily guarded. How do you expect me to light it?"

"Master Eric, are you not an aspiring dragon ace?"

# 40

The morning wore on and Isuthiel paced the cliff edge in front of the dragon hall. Azuria landed before him and paused to check the beach far below where Gernellian lay curled in the sand.

'Your time has come, Isuthiel.'

'Time?'

'The dragons of Dorcliff have long awaited a leader who can defeat Gernellian the Oppressor.'

'How? I've have failed once.'

'This time will be different.'

'Different? You have spent the past weeks healing him. He'll liquefy me in spit.'

'Isuthiel, I would never betray my nest mates. I would never betray Eric. You must attack Gernellian today. If you wait, he will kill me—and you will lose your advantage.'

'You've been caring for him—why would he kill you?'

'Please, trust me Isuthiel. I have broken most of the healer's rules to save the dragons. I go now to remove the poultices from Gernellian's talons. As soon as I do, you must attack, do not wait.'

"But he is much bigger and stronger than me."

*'He is not as strong as you fear. This task is yours, Isuthiel. May Eald D'Árian's finest blessings be upon you.'*

**************

Azuria's wings curled against the wind as she settled on the sand before Gernellian. She lowered her head in deference to the enormous wyvern.

*'Dragon! Why does my breath smell like a Gigag's stew pot?"*

*'It's the garlic, oh great one—I add it to your magma lozenges for its anti-inflammatory properties.'*

*'How much longer must I sit with my wing tucked up, suffering these confounded globs of muck on my talons and tail?'*

*'I have come today to remove them, your Majesty. Your magnificent wing is healed and so much faster than that of any inferior being I've known. I have brought one last dose of the magma lozenges if it pleases your Royal Magnificence.'*

*'Give them to me.'*

Azuria bowed her head as Gernellian gulped his doom.

*'Now take these accursed poultices from me, Dragon!'*

**************

High above the beach where Azuria tended the Golden Wyvern, Isuthiel paced and watched from a ledge. Talons sharpened, his muscles primed for battle. From this height, Gernellian seemed small but Isuthiel well knew the Wyvern's vast size.

*'Why has your sister betrayed us?'* The red dragon had returned each day to agitate as Azuria healed Gernellian.

*'I don't believe she has betrayed us.'*

*'You don't? Just look at her—'*

*'She has also been healing those Gernellian injured. She spends all her days caring for the sick—'*

*'Not long now, Isuthiel.'* Tenebrozi's head appeared over a nearby boulder. *'I will be close, if you need my help—I won't let you down.'*

*'This is a battle I must fight alone, Tenebrozi. Only if he kills me must you attack.'*

Far below, Azuria stepped away from Gernellian and bowed. Gernellian wafted the dry sand across the beach with his newly mended wing.

*'There! You see? She has healed his wing!'* The red hissed smoke down the cliff face.

Isuthiel focused his mind and plunged from the ledge as the wyvern lifted into the air. Down he sped with vigorous wing strokes; he adjusted direction to mirror the wyvern's path. Gernellian's wings stretched as wide across as Isuthiel's full length. Inspired by Tenebrozi's attack, Isuthiel punched a hole in Gernellian's wing, as he broke through, he caught a claw in the leathery membrane; the wyvern flapped and flicked him across the sand in a tangle of wings and tail. He sprang to his feet as the Wyvern roared and swooped; the torn wing propelled him off course. As his tail hit the sand, spikes and scales came free, scattering like leaves; as his feet touched down, the talons Azuria had moments ago unwrapped from the moss poultices detached and tumbled away to leave unprotected toes. Gernellian shrieked his fury, he curled his tongue over his snout and spat a thick glob of saliva, Isuthiel dived but the yellow blob hit his wing. It slid harmlessly to the sand. Again and again the wyvern hissed and spat, sticky saliva hung from his jaws. The more he spat, the thicker it grew, the weight dragged on his head. Isuthiel soared into the air and dived headlong into Gernellian's wing, biting and tearing. The wyvern swung his head, trying to dislodge the sticky yellow muck that clogged his jaws. Isuthiel leapt into the air. Gernellian flapped hard and lifted off the sand, Isuthiel looped and dived for the weakened wing bone; the crack resonated across the cliff face. The broken bone protruded from the leathery hide and the wyvern tumbled, screeching to the sand. Isuthiel wheeled, scudded to a halt before him and lunged—his fangs snapped and tore Gernellian's throat open. Wyvern blood sprayed across the sand.

*'Isuthiel! Get off the beach!'* Tenebrozi's panic-stricken voice reached him over Gernellian's death throes.

*'Quickly, Isuthiel.'* Azuria joined him. *'Hurry! Fly!'*

A rumble reached Isuthiel's ears; a vast cresting wave bore down on him. His muscles tightened, flexed and sprang, Isuthiel leapt and thrashed his powerful wings; the tidal wave crashed against the cliff base, flecks of foam chased him skyward. Isuthiel wheeled and swooped across the rushing water. The murderous brine slithered seaward bearing its prize—the shattered remains of Emperor Gernellian the Oppressor. Isuthiel roared flames of white and green across the spume. Crumpled wings and a red stain showed where his enemy's carcass drifted.

*'My humble gratitude, Azuria, may the blessings of Eald D'Ádrian be upon you. But how did you weaken him?'*

*'Tyrants like Gernellian become blinded by their power. Bow to them—flatter them and they'll assume you're spellbound by their magnificence. Knowledge of the earth and all its properties is one of the deadliest weapons of war. I have knowledge, Isuthiel, than can be wielded to lethal effect. I will now spend the rest of my days in atonement for the misuse of my birthright.'*

*************

*'Isuthiel—are you listening?'*

*'Eric! You're alive!'*

*'Yes. Is Tenebrozi sleeping? I need him to come for me.'*

*'Why not me, Eric?'*

*'Where I am, you have never been, Isuthiel. Tell Tenebrozi to come to Larkin's house.'*

*'Very well, Eric. I looked forward to your return, for I have great news.'*

*************

Onfroi's men who guarded the beacon tower gossiped and chewed jerky. Hoods pulled low, they hunkered out of the wind, none looked at the sky. Above them, the pile of oiled wood illuminated by the lighthouse's flame had not seen a blaze for many years. Generations of spiders had sheltered under the beacon's gable, weaving their traps, never knowing their doom was but a spark away. A whoosh brought the men to their feet as dark wings of a dragon materialised above. A long jet of flame roared from its mouth and the Oldegoth beacon lit for the first time that century.

The dragon rider called, "Take the rest of the evening off, gentlemen!"

# 41

The Crown Prince of Serasya's return to The Misty Isle might have gone unnoticed but for his company. The Gigag King, Gnogoly the Robust, dressed in his royal finery. With him, the Gigag Knights of Port Mortlock, mounted on red dragons, their shields bore the red, gold, blue and black of their country—colours repeated on the flag their herald carried. Their spears bristled skyward, broadswords and crossbows tapped their thighs; quivers brimming with arrows rattled on their backs. They landed in the square, outside the walls of the Royal Palace of Asyann. Serasyan courtesy demanded they give fair notice when arriving unannounced. The Gigag herald blasted long and loud on his bugle. A shaft of sunlight poked through the mist and illuminated the city long enough to bring the residents flooding from their houses.

The Gigag's herald waited until the streets filled then announced, "Good citizens of Asyann, the Crown Prince, Guidion di Larkyn has returned to Serasya! His Royal Highness, King Gnogoly of the Gigags has come with allegiance to the King in Waiting!"

The academic, Zildyr emerged from the palace and hurried to the gate.

"You there! Open that gate and grant the Prince and his party entry."

The people of the city cheered and bowed as Prince Guidion di Larkyn dismounted and assisted his bride from the dragon.

"The King is dead," the people chanted, "Long live the King!"

**************

The people's words caught Larkin's attention.

*The king is dead?*

At the top of the towers, the red and gold flags of his family and country flew at half-mast.

"Prince Larkyn, my boy! You have returned! Ryall, Aalys, my friends, this is indeed a pleasant surprise!"

Larkin embraced his childhood tutor. "Zildyr! It feels strange to return—I never intended to but in the past weeks, I have accepted it is my duty. Zildyr, what are the people saying?"

"Come inside, your Royal Highness, for I have grave news." Zylder bowed low to King Gnogoly. "Welcome to Asyann, your Majesty, King Gnogoly."

Larkin and his party followed Zylder through the gates. He gazed, bemused as the guards dropped to one knee, hand over heart they dipped their gaze.

*I'd forgotten how cowed and servile my father's subjects are.*

Up the wide stairs and through ornate doors Larkin never thought he'd see again.

"Your Highness, it is with regret I must inform you, your father passed away suddenly, yesterday morning

213

from apoplexy. It is propitious indeed, your return. Word arrived this morning; the King's men have opened the Golden Hall. Your brother's coronation is set to begin mid-afternoon, he is hopeful Inigo Thornfingers himself will arrive to crown him." Zildyr's moustache twitched and his eyes danced.

"Thornfingers." Larkin sighed.

Cateline held the crook of his arm as they followed Zildyr along the corridor to the great hall. King Gnogoly took Larkin's other side. Ryall and Aalys walked a step behind and ten Gigag knights brought up the rear. Larkin grimaced as he listened to Zildyr; when he'd decided to return, he had expected a fight with his father, the notion of fighting his brother troubled him.

"Well, you can cancel the coronation. I have returned to take my place as the King of Serasya—as much as it pains me to do so, I believe the future of the kingdom will be jeopardised if I do not."

"Many in the kingdom will be gratified to learn of your return, your Highness." Zildyr opened the door to the great hall and bade them enter.

The sight of his father laid out in his casket, the cruel face serene as if he took a nap, left Larkin with mixed feelings. He had intended to depose his father—shut him in a dungeon or even kill him if necessary but his father had absolved him of the task. Golden coins glimmered on his father's eyes and brought a wry smile to Larkin. Guidion di Dyum would naturally reject the traditional silver coins and choose gold, nothing but the finest for the arrogant King of Serasya.

Cateline's grip on his arm tightened as they approached his father's corpse, he detected a tremble in her hand.

"He cannot hurt you now, my love—even alive, he would not get near you."

King Gnogoly stood by his dead counterpart, bowed his head and rumbled words of respect.

A slither of metal on leather spun Larkin to face the door and push Cateline behind him. The distorted man cowering from the Gigag knights' swords brought a surge of affection and pity to Larkin's breast. Elyot's accompanying guards dropped their weapons and reached skyward, the Gigags held broadsword tips under their noses. He recognised his father's seneschal, Gilfalyn, older and greyer, standing beside Elyot.

*Gilfalyn. Guarding his own interests as always.*

Ryall and Aalys stepped in front of Larkin and obscured his view of Elyot.

"Elyot! My brother, it is good to see you." Larkin eased the Raigon-talth aside.

"You allowed her to die! You miserable—" Elyot's gaze swung to fix on a point next to Larkin. "But how?" His eyes flicked back and forth from Cateline to Larkin. "You—our father killed her!"

"Our father tried to kill her, I rescued her."

Elyot crumpled to his knees. "Cateline—forgive me, I failed you. How can I make it up to you?"

Cateline stirred Larkin's gallantry as she clung to his side, shrinking from the bent form of his brother.

Elyot clenched a trembling fist over his heart. "At any moment, our Lord Thornfingers will arrive to make me hale and hearty. Strong I will be, to rule Serasya—be my queen, Cateline, I beg you—"

"If you want to keep your head, little brother, you will not address my wife in such familiar tones. The responsibility of ruling Serasya is not yours, Prince Elyot so stand aside. I will grant you a title and fitting duties in due course but for now, I will have you return to your quarters and stay there until I send for you."

"Lord Thornfingers will come and—"

"If Thornfingers should arrive, I will bury his bones beside our father." Larkin nodded to the Gigag knights. "Lock my brother in his quarters."

The Gigags ushered the prince and his men into the corridor.

"Yield afterlings!" First Knight, Gnogiv's voice boomed. "Lead us to thine widdershins Prince's chamber and no fadoodle lest I graff ye with mine flachchet 'til ye quetch."

Larkin and Ryall accompanied Zildyr into the corridor to witness the knights escort Prince Elyot and his aids away; Zildyr smiled and murmured, "It has been too many years since I've had contact with Gigags. How is it they accompany you?"

"That is my doing, Zildyr," said Ryall. "King Gnogoly is a friend of the Raigon-talth. You know what romantics the Gigags are, he swore fealty on condition the Prince take a bride immediately. If Cateline of Oldegoth had not accompanied us you might be looking at a Gigag lass for Queen."

"Zildyr, can you gather my father's knights, guards, heralds, and available servants? I wish to talk to them."

"Certainly, please come and wait in the parlour and I will summon the kitchen to serve you and your party some refreshments."

**************

The all-pervading fog that plagued the Misty Isles thinned and planks of sunlight gilded the city of Asyann. Rarely seen blue sky splayed above and people poured into the streets for Sunfest.

The Heralds hurried through the crowds, their bells clanged and their voices rang. "Oyez, Oyez, Oyez! The Crown Prince of Serasya, Guidion di Larkyn has returned to Serasya! He bids ye, people of Asyann—one and all—to come before him!"

The bell-ringers across the city sweated and heaved, pealing a brassy melody to the pale blue plate above.

"Hear ye! One and all! A new age has arrived! The scheduled Coronation of Deputy Crown Prince Guidion di Elyot is cancelled." The Herald's voice cracked as he hustled up the steep street, "His Royal Highness, the rightful Crown Prince Guidion di Larkyn has returned to claim the Throne of Serasya!"

# 42

As Eric straddled Tenebrozi's shoulders, he listened, awestruck as his dragon related how Azuria and Isuthiel had defeated the Golden Wyvern. Unease at the plight of the children back in King's Port gnawed his gut. Below, monstrous waves rolled across the sea. The mist thickened and soaked Eric to his skin, water droplets stringed from the Tenebrozi's wings. After midnight, the southern coast of Dorcliff loomed before them and Tenebrozi soared upwards, away from the waves that crashed at its base. Gravel sprayed as he landed before the Dragon Hall, his wing-draft wafted leaves into the misty air.

*'Eric! I'm pleased you have returned!'*

Eric bowed. *'Your Majesty! Isuthiel Green-fire, Conquer of Dorcliff!'*

*'Please, Eric. I ask for no titles—only that the dragons can live in peace and liberty.'*

*'Where is Azuria?'*

*'She is performing her duty as the Healer of Dorcliff. Gernellian left many with injuries.'*

*'Where are Gernellian's remains?'*

*'Floating somewhere in the Parinith Strait—along with many of his kind.'*

*'Did you kill more than Gernellian?'*

*'No. Only him. The quake that toppled the Rock of Wycliff killed many; some arrived here and we moved them on to the Rock of Allor. The Wyverns must first prove they're peaceful before they're permitted on Dorcliff.'*

*'The Rock of Wycliff fell—is that why the sea is so rough?'*

*'I believe so, Eric. It is also why the mist gathers—the Brimstone Archipelago is erupting along its full length.'*

"Master Eric!" Gnoptly, dressed in a long nightshirt and woollen socks, tromped from the Dragon Hall. "Verily we welcome thee back to the fold. Ye snogged the hare's foot but come, Gnohog will fus a pot of crug for thee. Thou hast missed thine sister's nuptial hand-banding and knotting…"

"My sister's what?" Eric struggled with the rapid stream of Gigagian.

"…but heedless, thee will mark the crowning of His Nibs, Prince Larkyn. Ye must aweg at dagian's scrow."

"I—what?"

"Behold! Dringle nowt; wash and bellytimber for thee! Give me thine shreds, ye loom carked and drassocked." Gnoptly bustled into Tregaryon Hall and bellowed. "Gniwis! Gnohog! Prythee! Master Eric must wash, glop and yarken for the crowning!"

Eric smiled and wondered what Gnoptly planned to do to him; his smile vanished when the Gigag began tugging at his clothes.

"Now hang on, Gnoptly—"

"Prythee, Master Eric, nary be agruwed, for ye possess nowt I never seen. Ye'll be needing clean shreds to behold Prince Larkyn's coronation."

"But—"

"Tub for thee, young master."

"Oh, you want me to take a bath?"

**************

Washed and dressed in clean clothes, Eric tackled a bowl of delicious stew and bread. Gnoptly recounted Isuthiel's defeat of Gernellian.

"…thine blue queen, Azuria—she is revered by all on Dorcliff. She gave Gernellian the fungal rot and his ongles fell out. When Isuthiel frushed him, he blored and fnasted and then he phlegm-floshed himself. Then thine green dragon pinion-razed Gernellian and ragged his gizzards. Then he got wave dunked and we last saw him kee-kaw and carked in the sea. He quetched not long a'tall."

Eric sighed.

*I get your drift.*

# 43

Nutley waited, an hour ticked by and the bell in the kitchen tinkled with increasing urgency. His battered old face twisted in a smile as he sipped wine from a pewter cup. The bell tinkled, again. The usurper king's desperation evident with each flail of the clapper. Nutley drained his cup, squashed his hat onto his dome and hobbled into the passageway; the clunk of his hickory staff beat a slow syncopation to his shuffling steps.

"You rang, Prince Randolf?" Nutley wheezed and prised his bent frame into the parlour.

"Why don't you answer when I ring? Damn it! I'll not stand—"

"I am here, answering you, Prince."

"Prince? I'm the blasted King!"

"A blasted weasel is what you are." Though Nutley feigned an attempt at muted comment, he pitched his mumbles to reach Randolf's ears.

"I'll have your worthless head, Nutley! Keep your noxious little tongue behind your teeth!" Sweat dribbled down his grey face and beaded on his upper lip.

"It is with great risk I dare venture you need my worthless head to remain attached to my worthless shoulders, Prince Randolf."

"Don't call me Prince!" Randolf's voice cracked and caught in his throat; he croaked through clenched jaws. "Damn it, Nutley—please give me my medicine, please? I'm hurting all over—"

"It pains me not to say, it will come at some cost to yourself, Lord Randolf."

Randolf sobbed, "I'm the ki—" A grunt cut his words and his hands flew to his stomach. "Please—anything you ask—"

"The key to the keep is what I ask." Nutley hissed and narrowed his eyes. "The one you stole."

"I've lost it—please, Nutley, please?"

"No key—no medicine."

"Please! I don't know exactly—it's here somewhere, it's in a drawer—I don't know—those!" Randolf waved a shaking hand at his desk and fell to his knees. "Please!"

Nutley narrowed his pale eyes and produced the tiny glass vial from his pocket. Randolf snatched it with a shaking hand, the stopper popped sweetly and the Prince poured his daily dose of laudanum over the back of his tongue and swallowed. Nutley waited until Randolf's ragged breath eased to a whisper of dreamless sleep.

"Soon you'll get none, evil, devil spawn. Then you must face those demons you loosed upon your homeland." Nutley waved his hand, the drawers sprung open and he began to search for the key.

**************

With Cateline at his side, Prince Guidion di Larkyn took his place on the balcony that overlooked the palace gates and the square beyond. Four Gigag Knights, the Raigontalth, Zildyr, and the Archbishop of Serasya at their side.

The people of Asyann crowded in the forecourt and the square beyond for the first coronation in three decades.

**************

*'There it is! Tenebrozi—that's the palace, the grandest building in the city. Look at all the people, they gather for the coronation, I think.'*

*'Where should I land, Eric?'*

*'Swoop in and drop me at the front of the crowd and then fly up to the roof to wait.'*

Eric effected a perfect dive from Tenebrozi and touched the flagstones with weightless aplomb. Sabres scraped leather and he found himself gazing down the length of shining Gigag blades, one prickled his jaw.

"Hands in the air, oh gangly hoddypeak, or yarken to conk by mine flatchet!"

"Eric!" Cateline's voice called from the balcony above. Encircled by a dozen Gigags, Eric froze.

"Stand down, Gnogiv, he is the third Raigon-talth—though he has much learning to do." Ryall shouldered past the Gigags and clapped a hand on Eric's shoulder. "An entrance like that into the royal compound could easily get you killed, Eric Boy-Dragon, now come with me."

"I think they just wanted to shave my whiskers."

"You don't have whiskers yet, only bum-fluff." Eric stumbled on the flagstones as Ryall propelled him into the palace and up to the second level. "You're no use to us dead, Eric; from now on you go nowhere without my permission."

"Ryall, we need to do something. Tagrali is rounding up the children of Oldegoth and poisoning them with Wyvern venom—we've got to stop him!"

"Shush! Prince Larkyn is speaking."

"But—"

"We'll talk about it when this is over, now listen."

Eric clenched his fists, his jaw ached and his teeth hurt. He tapped his foot as the long ceremony to crown his friend Larkin the King of Serasya, dragged on; a clock in his mind ticked at pace with his heartbeat. While Serasya honoured its age-old tradition of coronation, evil marched through his home city, in the brown habit of monks. Eric saw the bent form of Larkin's brother, Prince Guidion di Elyot, attempt to speak to the grey-haired man beside him. The man shushed the younger Prince and gazed enthralled as the Archbishop of Asyann prayed over the kneeling figure of the King in Waiting. Nearby, the Gigag monarch boomed, "Verily!" after each sworn pledge.

**************

Cateline flung her arms around Eric's neck.

"Eric, you missed my wedding."

"Sorry, Sis. I bet it was a great do."

Larkin appeared at Cateline's side. "Eric, we missed you at our wedding."

Eric bowed. "Um—yes, I'm sorry, your Majesty."

"Stand up." Larkin patted his shoulder. "You and I were friends before I became King, and it is my wish that we will continue to be so. You have never bowed to me and I hope you never will. Ryall tells me there is a problem in King's Port—more urgent than the other problems."

224

"The situation there is a mess. The castle is sealed against all but those who can fly in on a dragon. Raulin is locked in the tower. Nutley has Randolf crocked on laudanum and all the servants are gone. The only people still in the castle are the knights, Randolf, and Nutley—and Raulin of course. Nutley is chief cook and butler—I don't need to tell you, that's not his ideal occupation."

Larkin smiled. "But it pleases me greatly to imagine the discomfit that would cause Randolf."

Eric tried to smile. "I assure you, Randolf is feeling no pain." As much as he hated what Randolf had done, he couldn't help but sympathise. "Randolf shut Onfroi out of the castle and now the knights refuse to allow it opened by any but themselves. They have left Randolf to the mercy of Nutley's deranged mind. But there is a terrible thing happening in Oldegoth and it's not Randolf's doing—well not directly. Hundreds of children from tots to mid-teens are being rounded up. They're going to be imbued with wyvern toxin and made into Wrygon-norce. Nutley thinks the monks have a pact with Tagrali, they've been supplying him with orphans—" Eric stopped at his sister's sob.

"Cateline, please do not let it distress you." Larkin's arms closed around his wife.

"That was why I took Eric and fled the orphanage. I saw them taking some boys, one fought them, said he didn't want to go." Cateline's voice faded to a whisper. "I saw him! I saw Tagrali! They poisoned that boy! I was so afraid they would take Eric—I had to get him out of there!"

Eric stared; his sister never had explained her resolve to stay away from the orphanage, now he understood.

"We have to do something; we have to stop him—"

"We will. Zylder, call the knights to convene in the great hall; between the Gigags and ourselves we can muster thousands, can we not? Recall the Heralds; we need able bodied men who are prepared to fight for the children of Eald D'Árian."

"Your Royal Highness!" A page appeared in the door and dropped to his knees. "With your permission, may I approach?"

Eric glanced at Larkin; the new King winced.

"Get to your feet, boy!" Larkin beckoned the boy to him. "Don't ever kneel to me again. You don't have to kneel to anyone."

The page gulped. "Please accept my apologies, your Majesty. This message just arrived from Castle Greycliff in the Kingdom of Oldegoth." He passed Larkin a grubby piece of parchment and backed away.

Larkin sighed, unfolded the missive and read aloud. "*'Hail King (or Prince) Guidion di Larkyn, ships bearing many hundreds of Wrigon-norce have been sighted, sailing to King's Port, they will be upon us within hours. We plead your assistance as we face the greatest threat to liberty and decency our world has seen. Your humble servant, Nutley.'* It seems we have little time to waste, Gentlemen."

Eric clenched his fists and teeth, the situation grew direr with each passing minute.

*What if we're too late to save all those children? Will we be too late to save King's Port?*

# 44

Larkin searched the upturned faces of the Serasyan and L'Áscarlien Warriors.

"I can see from some of your faces, you find my belief in the existence of Tagrali, laughable. I always doubted his existence myself until today when I heard of it from a reliable source. Of the continuing existence of Inigo Thronfingers I remain sceptical, but his disciples threaten the safety of the children of all Eald D'Ádrian. Eric of the Raigon-talth has seen with his own eyes, children marched through the streets in the city of King's Port."

The slabs of sunlight that glared through the windows winked out and the hall darkened. All eyes turned to the windows; the mood of the room grew sombre.

"It grieves me enormously that within a day of taking the crown I now must lead my people to war. The forces of evil that have arisen in Oldegoth will not be content to remain there. We have allowed Tagrali to continue his evil in the provinces of Bellcliff for many years, now the time has come to end it. We must remove him as the head of the Wrygon-norce—the ones he has created and indoctrinated. We must stop him from murdering many as he attempts to create more. The

Raigon-talth exists only for the betterment of our world; with a proper attention and guidance, I'm sure the Wrygon-norce can too.

"And so, fighting men of Serasya and L'Áscarle we must hasten now, to the capital of Oldegoth—"

"Behold! Ye Nibs Larkyn!" A Gigag burst in. "While ye metrop beeks, the wind faffles a flosh of roak to thine Kingdom and fetches a sloomy scrow!"

Larkin looked from the dripping Gigag to Ryall, seeking clarification.

"He says, 'While your city basks in the sun, the wind blows in a heavy fog and blacks out the sky.'"

"Your Majesty," Zildyr turned from a whispered conversation with another messenger to address Larkin, "A quake along the Brimstone Archipelago has caused increased volcanic activity, this is creating steam and releasing smoke and ash. Out to sea is the heaviest fog we have seen in many years, visibility has fallen a little over a dragon's length and that fog now creeps across Asyann. The Rock of Wycliff has fallen into the sea making giant waves and the ship your father sent forth on the morning of his death has sunk, there were forty soldiers of Serasya on board."

"What is your advice, Zildyr? Ryall?"

"I cannot see any option but to wait until the fog clears." Zildyr's voice dropped to reach only Larkin and Ryall's ears.

"Maybe not. Your Majesty, Eric has a Parinith Dragon's ability to see in almost pitch dark, he could lead us to King's Port."

Zildyr frowned. "We speak of the fifteen-year-old Raigon-talth?"

"Yes, he is immature and impulsive but I'd willingly trust him to lead us."

"Eric is trustworthy." Larkin nodded. "Ryall, prepare the men; we shall leave one hour hence. Zildyr, I must grant you the title of Steward of Serasya in my absence. My brother, Elyot is to stay in his tower until I return—I will not yet trust him with the rule of Serasya nor with the safety of my consort, Cateline."

Another messenger hurried dripping wet through the door and halted at the foot of the dais where Larkin, Ryall, and Zildyr stood.

The man bowed low, straightened and kept his eyes down.

"Your Majesty, if it pleases you, I have come with important news."

"Look at me." Larkin caught a glimpse of the man's eyes before he lowered them to chin-level. "Do not be afraid—I am not my father."

The messenger's tongue flicked across his lips.

Larkin frowned. "Tell me this news, quickly."

"Your Majesty, a man almost dead was washed up on the rocks in the province of Loigyn—west of here, last night. The physician who treated him sent me to give you this." The messenger's hand shook as he passed the scroll. Larkin broke the splotch of sealing wax and pulled the scroll straight.

*'Hail His Royal Highness, King Guidion di Larkyn.*

*A man who cannot remember his own name has washed up on our shores this evening. He says he is one of those your late king father sent to release Lord Thornfingers. He says they released the ghost of Lord Thornfingers who blasted them all into the ocean with hellfire; he parted the sea, shook the world, opened the furnaces of hell and blacked out the sky.*

*Your humble subject, Physician Milkyn.'*

Larkin chuckled and passed the parchment to Zylder. "I must try a stunt like that next time I appear at the Dragon Coliseum, no? It would guarantee my bonus."

"Should I tell your brother of this event?" Zylder examined the missive.

"Was it an event? I imagine if you are blown through the air by an explosion your mind might misconstrue much of what is flying alongside you, no? Tell him if you wish, in fact give him this scroll. I trust my brother enough to arrive at an intelligent conclusion. Tell him I want him to think things over and when I return my first duty will be to meet with him and discuss his role in the kingdom. Until then, he is confined to his tower."

# 45

Elspeth opened the oven to inspect the plump quails sizzling in the pan. Around them roast potatoes, pumpkin, and onions. Onfroi, Jacquelle, and Aldus would dine that night, a family dinner to discuss their latest setback. The invasion of the Wrygon-norce saw Onfroi's troops flee in the night. Elspeth sighed as she transferred the quails and vegetables to a serving platter. Since they hatched, she had fattened the quails on hemlock seeds and the delicious aroma of their baking flesh floated through the house. She served them with brown sauce and baked vegetables tossed with finely chopped rosemary, thyme, and hemlock leaves, Onfroi and his family would enjoy their final dinner.

*It is unwise to wound a witch...*

Back in the kitchen for a few minutes, Elspeth returned to the dining room with fresh table linen. As she laid them beside the diners, she listened to the polite argument in progress.

"My dear husband, may I make so bold to tell you, your actions have done the kingdom of Oldegoth immeasurable harm."

"Nonsense! King Randolf is just taking longer to adjust to his position then I expected." Onfroi spooned a roast onion into his mouth, chewed and swallowed. A sip of wine washed it down. "He is a capable young man—" he tore the juicy meat from a thigh. "—you'll see. Everything will work out."

Elspeth caught the truculent expression on Master Aldus's reddening face and smirked. *'Speak your doltish mind, oh young and aggrieved. Speak. Speak.'*

"Randolf is my brother, my lady Mother! Did you know that?"

"I beg your pardon, Aldus?"

Onfroi gagged on his wine; his cough turned to a hearty laugh. "The boy has had too much to drink! Young rogue!"

*'Speak the truth, young Aldus.'*

"I heard him say it, Mother! He told Randolf he is his son!"

"Onfroi? Is this true?'

The tingle of adrenaline raced through Elspeth's veins. "It is true, Lady Jacquelle."

"Out!" Onfroi poked a commanding finger at the door.

"Both of my sons that you sent to the monastery are also your husband's offspring."

"Oh my…" Lady Jaquelle's hand flew to her breast.

"Onfroi is a lying, adulterous murderer, Lady Jaquelle. Be grateful I used silphion, wild carrot, and pennyroyal to stop you producing any more of his children."

"You—"

"Yes, Elspeth the cook. Elspeth the witch! I cursed you barren. I cursed your son fatuous! I cursed Queen Elena to die in childbirth and her child with her! But Randolf didn't die. I'm not a good witch—I know just enough to be dangerous."

"Hush your common mouth, Elspeth! Go and pack your things, you are dismissed!"

A shriek of laugher rent from Elspeth's throat. "A dead man cannot dismiss anyone, my dear Onfroi!"

"What are you talking about, foolish woman?"

*...foolish to kill a wizard...*

"It is foolish to kill a wizard, Onfroi. Such a shame you killed the Wizard Hectar. Your greatest shame! There is an antidote to the poison you have all ingested tonight, Wizard Hectar could have administered it and saved you all, but you!" Elspeth's hand shook as she pointed at Onfroi. "You killed him! Like you killed our youngest son, Jerrold. Now you reap the spoils of your wicked deeds."

*...high treason to murder your King...*

Elspeth spat her denunciation.

"It is high treason to murder your king! You! Murderer! Strutting the streets of this city, thinking yourself above punishment for your scheming and evil! Your brutality! Your peccadillos and your lies! You promised me we'd be married but you came home with a bride and sent me to work in your kitchen—to bear you two illegitimate sons. You wanted your son to be king? Your son will be king, but not your favoured one! My son is Tagrali's chosen one! He will be King—the autocrat of Oldegoth and you and yours will be dead!"

"Please!" Lady Jaquelle's eyes rolled and foam bubble from her mouth. Aldus, who had bolted copious amounts of roast quail toppled from his chair, his kicks faded to twitches and he lay still. Onfroi's eyes bulged as he watched Lady Jaquelle slide to the floor. His mouth framed soundless pleas as he tried to rise. He slumped face down on his plate, his final breath gurgled bubbles in the brown sauce.

Elspeth moved around the table, her fingers groped for a pulse. Their hearts had stopped. She slipped the gold band from Lady Jaquelle's finger and squeezed it onto her own. She carried the plates to the kitchen and washed the dishes. As she worked, she whispered a prayer to her deity.

"Come forth, Lord Thornfingers and pass your Galiron Crown to my son."

The kitchen cleaned, she took a plate of leftovers from the oven and sat down to a meal of quail with roast potatoes and sauce.

# 46

The bunk grew cold as the night wore on. Raulin closed his eyes and willed his brain to stop its circular procession of worry. His stomach grumbled over the charred morsels he'd forced into it. The quality of the food pushed through the hatch had deteriorated in the past week and the castle had fallen silent. Even the seabirds' screeches had ceased; Raulin feared the world outside may have died. He woke to a red glow flickering through the high window of his prison; was his city burning? A cold mist drifted in, lit by the flames and dampness covered the hard surfaces of his tiny room high in The Keep.

*Is it because everything has fallen silent that I can hear the waves crashing? Or are the crashing waves the reason for that silence?*

The tower clock's midnight peal woke Raulin; he squirmed on the bunk and closed his weary eyes. Tormented dreams of poisonous fog and daggers abraded Raulin's sleep; monstrous seas pounded the ramparts like drums of war. His eyes snapped open as his overwrought brain jolted him awake again. He grimaced at the glow through the window and rolled onto his side. A loud click brought him properly awake; the door creaked and the yellow flicker of a candle penetrated the darkness.

Raulin's feet found the floor; he edged against the wall and waited. A clunk of wood and a scape of leather sandals shuffled over the flagstones.

"Nutley! How did you get past the guards?"

"Your Majesty!" Nutley wheezed and gasped. "You startled me so my bowels all but evacuated themselves."

"What's happening, Nutley? Why is it so quiet? And what is burning? Where is my brother, has he sent for me? I'll kill him with my bare hands so help me—"

"One question at a time, your Royal Highness. Evil is happening. It's quiet because your servants had it too good under your reign." Nutley tilted his head as he pondered the questions before him; his pale eyes gleamed in the reddened shadows. "The beacons are lit; I subdued your brother and recovered the key to the Keep. We wizards await your instruction, King Raulin."

"Where are the other wizards?"

"Milo, Giles and Calder expect you in your parlour, your Majesty. Wischard, Ferrick, and Hawser haven't returned yet, they set out the day after Castle Greycliff fell to gather Oldegoth's warriors."

"What of Sir Cesper and his knights? Where are they?"

"Cesper assured me they all remain in the castle and loyal to Oldegoth, Sire."

"That is a small comfort at least, Nutley; I will speak to them at my first convenience. Have my ships returned to the harbour yet?"

"No Sire. Their whereabouts is unknown."

"That is grave news. Where is my brother?"

"We have transferred him to his own parlour and locked him in."

"How? Where are Onfroi and his men?"

"Randolf exploded and ordered Onfroi to leave the castle after the servants walked out. He ordered the drawbridge closed and now the knights won't allow it opened. Onfroi's men had maintained siege to the city until an hour ago when they fled along with many of the city's folk in the face of a more dangerous enemy."

"And which enemy is that?" Raulin worried, if just forty knights remained in the castle, how would he defend it? "What of Gilda and the Elite Guard? Where are they?"

"All dead, Sire. Gilda was betrayed by Tomas…" Nutley told Raulin of the treachery and betrayal of that night.

"… now Failed Wizard Tagrali has arrived with a seething horde of Wrygon-norce, I abandoned my efforts to count them, Sire, but I estimate two hundred score."

Raulin's skin crawled.

*Four thousand!*

Parents of Eald D'Árian raised their children to fear Tagrali and they carried that fear into adulthood. "Where is he? Where are they?"

"In the square and around the edge of the mote, your Majesty, along with many hundreds of children captured from all over Eald D'Árian. They haven't attacked yet, perhaps their plan is to starve us out."

Raulin rested his head against the stones and gazed at the mist floating in the window. "You didn't say how you subdued Randolf—how did you lock him in his parlour?"

"Sire, the pressure of running a Kingdom weighed heavily on your brother and he found succour in your vast wine collection. When he had ingested it all he searched for something more."

"And you gave it to him, didn't you, Nutley?"

"I did, Sire, I did. Now come, your Majesty, and convene the first wizard gathering in ten years." Nutley tugged Raulin's hem.

As Nutley led him into the room, Raulin smiled. Milo, Giles, and Calder gained their feet, bowed and applauded.

"My friends, it is gratifying indeed to see you gathered together after all these years." Raulin scanned the room and sniffed the air. "Do I smell Milo's meatloaf?"

"You do indeed, your Majesty." Milo carried a covered dish to the table. "Tuck in Raulin; I believe it has been some time since you ate a decent meal. Nutley's cooking has killed more men than the sharpest battleaxe."

"I am an apothecary—not a cook." Nutley scraped and clunked across the room, sat and wheezed.

***************

Elspeth lay dying from her last meal. On her left hand, the ring Onfroi denied her long ago. Her surviving son, born of unrequited love had made Elspeth proud. Strong and handsome—embued with wyvern toxin. Tagrali's chosen one.

"Elspeth!"

Elspeth opened her eyes to her lifelong friend, Marsie.

"I'm dying, Marsie. Remember me with fondness."

"No, you're not dying—I won't let you."

"I killed them all, Marsie."

"Hush, Elspeth. You did no such thing, they were accidentally poisoned. Hush now, here comes the physician."

Elspeth's eyes dimmed; the room went black.

**************

In the southern streets of King's Port, as far possible from Castle Greycliff, Harald the Herald rang the Dead Bell.

"Oyez—Oyez—Oyez! Pray listen, good citizens of King's Port! The good and gentle Onfroi, and the Lady Jaquelle are dead! Master Aldus has died beside them! Hear ye! Onfroi is dead!" Harald flailed his bell and checked behind him; silence ruled this end of King's Port. "Oyez! Oyez! Since my words fall upon empty streets, may I make so bold as to venture that Onfroi is dead, may he rot in the dirt; may Eald D'Árian remember his duplicity and hurt. He, his lady, and their misbegotten pup; their death may we toast with an overflowing cup!"

Harald the Herald sniggered. He fancied himself quite a poet.

He turned, the clop of hooves echoed in the mist and a mule-drawn cart rattled and squeaked over the cobblestones towards him. Harald withdrew into a doorway and squinted at the black-cloaked driver, the long weathered hands that grasped the reins the only evidence of a human underneath. The mule turned down an alley and headed west, pulling the little cart onto a narrow road out of the city.

Harald shivered. "There's some strange folk abroad this afternoon."

**************

The wooden cart bounced behind the mule, past the last buildings and through the shanties on the city's outskirts; the driver's black hood bobbed along the length of the stone walled lane and the little mule snorted with exertion as it trotted up the hill and turned west onto Castlebridge Road away from the city.

The cloaked man met another riding a pony towards him out of the mist. "Hail, Ferrick my friend!"

"Wischard! How was your mission?" Ferrick and Wischard both turned through the wrought iron gates of Mystmere, along the gravel road and stopped before Larkin's manor.

Wizard Hawser greeted the new arrivals as he unharnessed the pony from his sulky. "You're just in time, Bretheren—the enemy is on our doorstep."

"Oldegoth shall fight—"

"When the beacons ignite."

"Indeed! Indeed! Come, the King, and the head of our order await us."

# 47

The head and eyes of the beast, Eric led the throng of dragon riders into the murk. The grim faces behind him blackened in the smoke and ash suspended by the fog. Enormous wings susurrated through the mist across the Serasyan Sea. They carried no banners; few wore the regalia of their King—only the Knights of L'Áscarle and Serasya wore a warrior's raiment. Each flew with King Guidion di Larkyn's words ringing in their ears.

"Men of L'Áscarle and Serasya, today we face a choice, remove Tagrali from the world or forever suffer his evil."

Ryall, Aalys, and Eric had welcomed King Larkyn's personal order.

"Kill Tagrali—cut off the head of the serpent whose venom threatens our world."

Far below Eric, the Brimstone Archipelago glowed in the mist, away to his right the dark mass of Dorcliff Island loomed. He reached out with his mind and touched Azuria and Isuthiel—a wish for their peace and happiness should he not return. Minutes later, he caught a glimpse of the Oldegoth beacons lambent in the mist. Two fires close together would be the beacon and the lighthouse of King's Port; their flickering light guided him home.

"King's Port ahead!" he called over his shoulder to Ryall.

Ryall's voice sounded in the minds and ears of the cohort. "Each of you has memorised the layout of King's Port and you have your instructions. Fight bravely men of Eald D'Árian! For the children of our world and for King Raulin the Redeemer!"

Eric smiled at the roars of the men behind him.

**************

Cesper's boots resounded in the deserted corridor, he checked room after deserted room—he tried the door to the King's quarters—locked. Prince Randolf's—locked. He poked his head into the kitchen and frowned. To the vestibule and through to the Great Hall, Castle Greycliff stood cold and deserted. The Keep remained locked.

*Is the King still up there?*

"Nutley!" He listened to his voice reverberate in the silence. "Nutley?"

The bent old man who cared for the greenhouses had disappeared, along with Randolf. Cesper grabbed a torch from the wall and hurried down the stairs to the dungeons. His skin crawled in keeping with the occupants—rats and bugs—no humans. This didn't bode well. Back upstairs, Cesper took an axe to Randolf's parlour door. Deserted. The King's door took longer to hack through.

"I might have saved my energy." He searched the King's parlour, bedchamber and library.

*Where did they go? How did they escape?*

# 48

Tagrali stood on a plinth beside the Castle Bridge and congratulated himself. At his feet a cloaked figure sat, arms hugging its knees, head bowed and face hidden. Before him gathered his life's vocation. For years he had harvested children, humans from Oldegoth and Serasya, slokks from Belcliff, and gigags from the Isle of L'Áscarle. He imbued them with the acid of a wyvern hatchling, most died but those who survived grew tall and strong. He favoured the slokks of Belcliff Island for his Wrygonnorce; fiercer than humans and gigags, their long, sinuous limbs gave them strength and speed. Tagrali preferred small children; their malleable minds absorbed his teachings without dispute. His fervent belief in the ancient, rambling texts of Inigo Thornfingers justified his actions. The dragons had ever been his strongest foe but his pact with Gernellian the Oppressor, Emperor of Dorcliff, had seen the dragons brought to heel—their reduced and aging population posed little threat to his plan.

He admired his purpose-built army; each soldier carried a trident, the symbol of Lord Inigo Thornfingers, and the brand on each forehead. He'd lost count but estimated he had around three thousand fighters—not highly trained but their size, strength, and zeal made them a formidable foe. The spares huddled behind them, children waiting for their imbuement—the Wrygon-norce in in the making.

Tagrali thundered through the mist to his soldiers. "Fellow disciples! Lord Thornfingers has sent us this vapour to blind our enemies and allow us to take Oldegoth for his divine purpose!"

The Wrygon-norce answered as one. "Lord Thornfingers has spoken and we shall obey!"

"He commanded the dragons to withdraw their allegiance from Oldegoth and they have returned to their native land where they serve the mighty Gernellian!"

"Lord Thornfingers has spoken and we shall obey!"

"The tide has turned, the humans stand divided!"

"Lord Thornfingers has spoken and we shall obey!"

"We—the venin-born, shall strike down the non-believers, defeat Lord Thornfingers' enemies and take his Galiron Crown for our chosen King."

"Lord Thornfingers has spoken and we shall obey!"

"Lord Thornfingers, God of Eald D'Arian!"

He bared his teeth in a satisfied grin as the Wrygon-norce roared in mindless benediction. "Lord Thornfingers has spoken and we shall obey!"

While the volcanic steam shrouded Eald D'Árian he would take Castle Greycliff, the greatest fortress ever built, and install his foremost disciple as King. When the forces of men challenged, the Wrygon-norce would defy them from behind mighty walls.

"When the fortress of Castle Greycliff falls, so shall the Kingdom of Oldegoth!"

"Lord Thornfingers has spoken and we shall obey!"

The drawbridge cracked open, the chains rattled and hinges squeaked as it sank to span the moat. The

Wrygon-norce cheered and roared. Many leapt before the drawbridge had fully lowered. They ran up the winding streets towards the Keep, tridents of steel clutched in their fists and murder in their hearts.

**************

The sight of a seething horde crossing the drawbridge and inside the walls of Castle Greycliff sent Eric's heart into his throat.

"They've taken the Castle! We're too late! What can we—"

"Take heart, Eric—we have dragons and well-trained men!" Ryall steered Ryzolth to fly beside Tenebrozi. "We came here to fight. Instead of fighting them in the streets, we'll fight them in the fortress."

The fog billowed in the draft of dragon wings as they swooped. Larkin's soldiers settled in the square. The Gigag and Serasyan knights directed their dragons over the wall and into the fortress—through the streets their screeches mingled with the shouts of their riders and echoed off the walls. Dragon fire licked the enemy. Eric, Ryall, and Aalys peeled off, their fight lay elsewhere.

**************

Trudging along the Castlebridge Road, King Raulin's serving staff, Yrian at the centre, formed a grim line behind the Knights of Oldegoth led by Sir Dowden. A peasant army followed. A rag-tag mob united from across the kingdom advanced on Castle Greycliff to answer the beacon's call. Men who had marched with Onfroi just weeks before changed allegiance when faced with

Tagrali's fearsome army; they united under King Raulin's grey and black flag.

"Charge!" A bullnecked man with ram's horns on his helm led the first platoon across the drawbridge to clash with the Wrygon-norce. "We fight for King Raulin! Charge!"

Lucretia, Balien and their fellow aces sailed over the wall on a blaze of dragons and attacked with spears and dragon fire.

In the square, King Guidion di Larkyn and his soldiers dismounted to form a circle around the shackled children. Others advanced on the Monks of St Saxxa who sat guard.

"Back you evil curs!"

"Remove those chains," King Larkyn called to his men. "Follow me, we'll take them to the Coliseum!"

The Monks abandoned their post and fled, the mothers of Oldegoth chased brandishing axes, knives, rolling pins, brooms, and clubs. The Monks' sandalled feet raced over the cobblestones along Silversage Street.

"Our children are sacred!" Marsie shouted as she led the pursuit. "You abandoned your faith and your vows to follow evil!"

"Burn them out!"

"Let's rid our world of this canker!"

"Strike down this evil pestilence!"

"Burn the monastery!"

**************

Raulin paced the drawing room in Larkin's house; the fog beyond the windows isolated him from the world.

"For heaven's sake, Calder! Let me go and assist my people."

"There is no need, your Majesty—Nutley assures me the Raigon-talth have arrived with a powerful army. Wischard, Ferrick, and Hawser have rallied many. The peasants of Oldegoth have united under your flag; even those who fought for Onfroi have returned their allegiance to you."

"I must fight—how can I look my people in the eye and call myself their King if I stay here, hiding, while they fight my battle?"

"The people know the value of their King. They don't expect—"

"Calder, if you don't allow me through the tunnel, I will take the road. One way or another, I will fight for my kingdom. I would rather begin that fight from inside the castle."

"Your Majesty—"

"Are you going to unlock that door?"

"But your blood is—"

"My blood is the same colour as my people, Calder—if it is spilled—if I die, there will be someone to replace me."   Raulin buckled his sword belt, his eyes narrowed. "Let me through the tunnel, Reeve Calder, that's an order."

"Very well, Raulin, but you will suffer me at your side for the whole exercise."

"What better ally could I ask for than a wizard? I wouldn't have it any other way, my friend."

# 49

Eric, Ryall, and Aalys landed their dragons in the bailey of the Elite Guard in their search for Tagrali. Eric held Tenebrozi's reins and searched for Tagrali with his mind, his conscience bounced off the dry walls of the Wrygonnorce's collective psyche—a single ambition to serve Lord Thornfingers. He pushed and moved on. Softness touched his mind—blue eyes filled with tears and a heart full of sorrow.

*'Clarice?'* Sadness dragged on Eric's mind and he fell. He hit the ground, his mind burst open and a harsh voice hammered in his head.

"Eric!" Someone smacked his cheek. "Eric! Come back to us."

Eric sat up and brushed tears from his eyes. "Clarice—she's alive!"

Ryall cupped Eric's face between his hands. "Eric, calm down and relax your mind. You opened yourself to Tagrali—he's an expert scrier."

"I have to find her, Ryall, she's in trouble! I think Tagrali has got her."

"Yes, I think he has too and he is going to use her to bring you to him. You must empty your mind of emotion. Your feelings for her will get you killed."

"Look out!" Aalys's terror conveyed Eric to his feet, sword in hand. A pack of Wrygon-norce poured into the bailey and pounced. One leapt at Eric, trident raised. Eric dodged and slashed. Aalys's dragon, Lymelzia screeched, her flames enveloped another Wrygon-norce, her lashing tail fell him at Aalys's feet—she swung and stabbed. A monstrous scream filled the bailey and the trident clanged on the stones. An enemy lunged, his trident knocked Eric's sword from his hand. Eric dived and rolled. The trident stabbed, sparks strew across the stones. Eric snatched the dropped trident and speared his attacker's throat. The metallic scent of blood mingled with singed hair and burning flesh. Ryzolth's jaws clamped over the head of a Wrygon-norce, he flung him over the bailey wall. Eric's heart pounded, his muscles bunched. A monstrous Wrygon-norce bent as he ran through the arch towards him, one fist carried a trident, the other swung a flail.

"This way—let's go!" Ryall mounted Ryzolth. Eric and Aalys scrambled onto their dragons to follow. The Wrygon-norce swung the flail, it tore Eric's sleeve; Tenebrozi shot flames at the huge head.

As they pulled level with the tower roof, Ryall's voice sounded in the mist. "Eric, can you see anyone? It should be two people, possibly three—I sense a third obstructing from the shadows."

As Eric circled on Tenebrozi, shouts, screams, rattles and clangs of weapons rang in the mist below. A battle raged through the streets of Castle Greycliff as humans, Gigags, and dragons clashed with the Wrygon-norce. The beacon fire gilded the fog as they circled the towers; Eric searched the shadows.

"There! There! Someone is down there on the wall."
Anger and the urge to kill soared, Eric's head filled with
laughter and screaming.

"Eric, focus!" Ryall's voice pulled him back. "Calm
your mind."

Eric straightened in his saddle, inhaled and allowed
Ryall's mind to touch and calm his. Tenebrozi settled on
the wall and Eric slid off to stand beside him. Three
yards wide, the fortress wall had battlements on the
outer edge. Waves crashed far below on the seaward
side. On the inside the clashes, shouts, and screams of
battle continued in the streets of Castle Greycliff. Ahead
two people stood shrouded in the mist, a tall, cloaked
figure, eyes glowed in its cowl. Its hand rested on the
shoulder of a smaller figure, her blond hair clung to her
face.

"Clarice, I'm glad to see you—"

"She cannot hear you, Eric Man-dragon. I rule her
mind—she hears only what I allow. She has become a
Wrygon-norce, like you."

"I'm not a Wrygon-norce—" Eric fell to his knees,
laughter exploded in his head—Clarice's terror filled his
heart.

"Eric!" Aalys's voice dragged him back. "Calm your
mind."

Eric sprang to his feet. His sword raised. Ahead, Ryall
advanced on the figure in the black hood, a yellow
fireball erupted and engulfed the elder Raigon-talth—his
laughter rang from the inferno.

"You'll need more than fire to stop me, Failed Wizard
Tagrali!" Ryall brushed the flames aside and step closer.
Tagrali raised a dagger to Clarice's throat and dragged
her to the wall's edge.

Eric fixed his mind on hers. *'Clarice—can you hear me?'*

A blank space greeted him.

*'Clarice! Let me in—I'm Eric—your friend.'*

A flicker.

*'Clarice?'*

Eric sensed Clarice's mind waking.

*'Keep it up, Eric—Ryall is keeping Tagrali busy.'* Aalys encouraged.

*'Clarice, listen to me—'*

"Get down, Eric!"

Eric twisted at Aalys's warning, a Wrygon-norce towered over them, its yellow eyes glowed through the mist. Tenebrozi sprang, swung his tail and sent the Wrygon-norce over the battlements to the sea-swept rocks far below. The quarterstaff clunked and bounced to the stones, Eric snatched it up and returned his mind to Clarice.

*'Clarice—remember when you helped train me for the Elite Guard?'*

# 50

Ryall's head hurt as he delved and pummelled Tagrali's conscience. *I'll need to scrub my mind when this is over.* He renewed his focus.

'*What do you mean, he is Wrygon-norce?*'

Crazy laughter faded in the void and Ryall pushed harder.

'*What do you mean?*'

'*My most faithful servant—my chosen one—imbued him as they took him to the dungeon. Eric Man-dragon is Wrygon-norce! He is mine!*'

'*I don't believe you—how was a servant of yours in Castle Greycliff?*'

'*He has been here for years, pretending to serve the heathen King but all the while, he has served me.*'

'*A sleeping snake, eh?*' Ryall split his conscience. '*Ryzolth—are you ready?*'

'*I am, Master Ryall.*'

Blocked from Tagrali, part of Ryall's mind followed the dragon as he slipped from the wall, flung his wings wide, and circled.

'*Eric Man-dragon is a Raigon-talth—his dragon blood is the strongest we've seen.*'

'*He is also Wrygon-norce—does that disappoint you, Ryall Man-dragon?*'

*'I can live with it. Thornfingers himself was a Raigon-talth.'*

*'The dragons banished He and Gralix! Their extinction is their punishment. They are a dying race— the Golden Wyvern has all but eliminated the wild dragons of Dorcliff. Then it will me mine—a nation of Wrigon-norce! Part of the new kingdom of—'*

*'The dragons are stronger than ever, thanks to Eric Man-dragon.'*

*'How so?'*

**************

Eric halted beside Ryall, his mind and eyes fixed on Clarice.

*'Clarice, catch the staff!'*

Ryzolth swooped and blasted flames at Tagrali. Eric tossed the quarterstaff. Clarice grabbed at it and missed. The wizard fell from the wall and dragged her with him.

Eric's heart leapt as a purple flash lit the mist. He jumped and landed on the flagstones below, the quarterstaff bounced beside him. Clarice remained suspended. Shuffle, clunk, Nutley emerged from the mist; one hand clutched his staff the other outstretched, a jagged, twisting beam of purple light held Clarice aloft. He lowered her to the cobblestones.

She lived, her chest heaved. Eric ran to her.

The warriors' shouts grew louder as the battle for Castle Greycliff edged nearer.

Tagrali clambered to his feet and advanced. "She is mine—"

"The hell she is!" Sparks flew in the dark as Eric's sword dashed the dagger from Tagrali's hand; it clattered away in the dark. "Stay back lest I'll cut your throat!"

Nutley halted beside Clarice. "Do it, Master Eric—cut his unworthy throat. Failed Wizard Tagrali must die."

Eric glanced at the bent form of Nutley as he knelt beside Clarice and placed his hand on her forehead; eyes squeezed shut, his lips framed a silent incantation.

"Do it, Eric!" Ryall's feet hit the stones beside him.

Eric drew back and prepared to plunge his sword into Tagrali.

"I can't let you do that, Eric." Sir Cesper emerged from the shadows and stepped in front of Tagrali. His sword glinted.

Nutley wheezed to his feet, his eyes gleamed as they fixed on Sir Cesper.

A shiver of fear dance down Eric's spine. "What are you doing, Cesper? He's evil—he must die!"

"He is my lord—the only one I serve. I am Tagrali's chosen one."

"Sir Cesper?" Nutley croaked. "But you serve our King Raulin—he made you his first knight!"

A memory flashed in Eric's mind. A tall, cloaked figure in the shadows. He recalled Sir Cesper's words on that night, months before.

*'One of my informants—there is more to being a knight than—'*

"No, Sir Cesper has never served Raulin, have you Cesper?" Anger surged, laughter cackled in his head.

*'Come unto me, Eric Man-dragon—find your true destiny.'*

A warm embrace enveloped Eric's mind—he rejoiced at joining Tagrali.

*'That's right, Man-dragon—give up your soul to Lord Thornfingers'*

Happiness filled him—he would belong somewhere—he'd have a home, the love of a parent. Clarice would be there. One hundred fists pounded in the orphan's chest, euphoria flooded his veins.

*'Yes—my Lord Thornfingers—'*

*'Eric! Remember who you are, you are Raigon-talth, Eric Man-dragon.'* The strength of Ryall's mind jolted Eric. The euphoria shattered and reality returned. His hand tightened on the sword held at Cesper's throat. His hatred and fear of Tagrali resurfaced.

Eric inhaled, his head throbbed. "You are a traitor, Cesper. A dirty, filthy traitor!"

Cesper's amber eyes glinted and his face darkened. "No, I could only be a traitor if I truly served King Raulin. I have always served Tagrali and worshipped my Lord Thornfingers who chose me to lead the Wrygon-norce. Come to us, Eric. I made you a Wrygon-norce so you could join us—be on the right side of history. You, I, and Clarice are the unbranded ones; together we will find glory—"

Anger surged at Cesper's suggestion and the warm embrace returned; Eric's legs shook.

"No! Never! And I won't let you take Clarice!"

The laughter in his head returned and increased; screams and shouts—children cried and pled for mercy. Bruising pain throbbed as Eric's knees hit the flagstones.

*'You are mine, Eric Man-dragon!'*

"Come back, Eric—listen to me!" Aalys's arms enveloped Eric's shoulders. "Shut him out, Eric!"

Eric inhaled and shook his head. Beside him, Ryall continued his telepathic attack on Tagrali, his relaxed faced twitched—his neck trembled. Eric saw Cesper's lip curl as he advanced on the elder Raigon-talth and raised his sword. From the depths of his trance, Ryall parried, Cesper's eyes widened. Ryzolth advanced with teeth bared, his chest glowed and sparks peppered from his mouth; the knight backed away.

A roar startled Eric to his feet; the monstrous Wrygon-norce had found them, his head blistered and smouldered from Tenebrozi's fire. He swung the chain-flail, Aalys screamed and leapt aside. In his peripheral vision, Eric saw Clarice gain her feet to swing the quarterstaff at Cesper. Tenebrozi swooped and scorched the enormous Wrygon-norce. The chain-flail swung a full circle in a direct arc at Ryall's head. A streak of lightening flashed and crackled. Sparks flew from the flail as it stopped mid-air and glowed red-hot, the heat flowed up the chain to the Wrygon-norce's arm and he erupted in flames. Eric turned, the lightening came from the stones under Nutley's feet, radiated through his body and outstretched hands; the wizard shuddered, his eyes rolled back in his head and his face twitched.

"Nutley!"

Nutley's hands dropped to his side and he collapsed to the cobblestones. The huge Wrygon-norce fell in a blazing heap, acrid smoke billowed into the mist. The molten flail crashed to the ground, it sparked and fizzled over the wet stones.

Eric and Aalys sprang to their feet to defend their leader as he battled wits with Tagrali. Cesper's menacing amber eyes blazed in the gloom as he advanced on Clarice. Eric swung his sword. Cesper parried. Eric lost his grip, the sword clanked to the stones. Aalys charged past Eric and locked blades with Cesper. Eric lunged, smashed his fist into Cesper's face and blood spurted from his nose.

Gleeful shouts filled the air as King Larkyn, King Raulin, King Gnogoly, and a horde of warriors raced towards them.

"Behold!"

"Eric!" Yrian's voice reached him over the din.

"Victory is ours!"

Gnogoly's voice boomed. "Givel the gallybaggers and fang them with dragon-fire!"

Nutley coughed and prised himself upright with his staff.

"You've lost, Sir Cesper," the old wizard advanced, trembling violently. Eric listened to him wheeze and feared for Nutley's life. "Tagrali's purpose-built army is defeated. The children will reunite with their families. Behold that glow in the mist. The Monastery is a-blaze, the mothers of Oldegoth have spoken—Failed Wizard Tagrali and his chosen one are not welcome here!"

A hissing stream of yellow smoke spiralled, obscuring Tagrali and Cesper. Ryall and Eric lunged into the acrid cloud, their swords slashing and cutting sinew and bone. Tagrali fell, blood streamed from his lifeless body and the yellow smoke drifted in the mist. Cesper's sword clanged to the stones as Eric pinned him beside his leader.

"Are you going to kill me, Eric?"

"Give me one reason why I shouldn't."

"You and I are brothers, Eric—Clarice is our sister."

"I think Tagrali's smoke trick has clouded your brain, Sir Cesper—you are garbling."

"We are venin-born brothers—we both became Wrigon-norce from the precious venom my master collected from the great Gernellian's infancy. Gernellian is mightier than the dragons—his Wyvern blood is superior to a dragon's."

"What makes you think Gernellian is mightier than the dragons?"

"He has ruled them for eighty years, they can never challenge him—they're too small and weak."

"It will dismay you then to know the same dragon that gave me my venin blood killed Gernellian not three days ago."

"No! You lie—"

"His carcass floats somewhere in the Parinith Strait."

"No! No! I don't believe you."

"Tough. And now I get to kill you."

Eric's hand tightened on his sword.

*Do I want to take the life of an unarmed man? Become an executioner? Cesper is a victim of Tagrali's evil as much as the smallest child chained in the square.*

"Or perhaps I'll let the King decide your fate."

People crowded around, Sir Kilburn, and Sir Albiron, moved to stand either side of Eric.

"Thank you, Eric Man-Dragon." Sir Kilburn patted Eric's shoulder. "We'll take charge of Cesper."

"What will you do with him?"

"He will face a charge of treason. It is for the King to decide his punishment."

"He needs a physician."

"As do many who have suffered because of his treachery."

Eric turned away. Others would decide Sir Cesper's fate.

"Eric!" Clarice ran at him.

"Clarice, are you hurt?"

"I'm not!"

Eric's joy overflowed as Clarice flung herself into his arms. He held her close, her warmth stole into his heart. She remained in his embrace for a moment then pulled away.

He studied her face, pale with shadows under her eyes. "Yes, you are, you're hurt. Tagrali has wounded many, but I am here and no one will hurt you again."

"Eric, we must remember our place."

"Clarice—"

A smile softened Clarice's eyes. "Give it time, Eric. We are young and we are all that remain of the Elite Guard."

"Not all."

Eric turned at the familiar voice. "Haman?"

"Yes, Eric. Haman."

Haman had grown taller and heavier, his eyes glowed amber and a festering trident brand oozed on his forehead.

"I may be a Wrygon-norce, but I am not and never was Tagrali's."

# 51

In the light of dawn, the people of Oldegoth converged on King's Port. Hundreds searched for stolen children. Families sought loved ones who had fought for their King and country. Glad cries of reunion mingled with wails of anguish. The fog lifted to watery sunshine, the seabirds recommenced screeching as they swooped over the choppy waves of King's Port Harbour.

To Eric, Castle Greycliff was an open wound, slowly draining and healing as wagonloads of dead, enemy fighters seeped from the drawbridge and creaked away into the countryside. The warriors of Oldegoth, L'Áscarle, and Serasya toiled to clean the wound, removing the fallen and healing the ancient fort. In the distance, Balien and Lucretia knelt beside an injured dragon and applied a salve to a freshly stitched wound. As Eric helped the knights move the dead, he saw King Gnogoly the Robust, sitting on a block of broken masonry. He sang a victory song while Milo stitched a gaping wound on his face. Eric grinned as Milo joined the final chorus.

"…and the brave, straight-fingered knights march home and the vanquished are givelled in the ha-ha trench!"

The morning wore on and thousands gathered in the city square at the foot of Castle Greycliff. Eric's love for his King misted his eyes as Raulin climbed to stand on the back of a dragon statue, accompanied by King Gnogoly and Larkin. Like all who survived, Raulin's face bore the marks of battle—scratches, bruises, soot, blood and muck. He waved the cheering crowd to silence. His solemn eyes scanned the faces before him.

"My people! Let me thank you with all my heart for your loyalty and bravery. I hope you will all take the time to give thanks to King Gnogoly and the Gigag Knights of Port Mortlock, and to King Guidion di Larkyn, the Serasyan Knights and volunteers who came to our aid. I pray these old friendships will endure long into the future."

He paused and smiled at the crowd's acclamation. Many King's Port residents stared in wonder; a familiar local, Larkin the Dragon Ace now wore the crown of Serasya.

"This victory belongs to all, as does our sorrow for those lost and maimed. I pledge before you, my continuing dedication to your freedom and well-being. I ask you not to punish your neighbour for previous disloyalty; mistakes have been made by many including myself. We must work together and repair the damage done. I plead with you all to help me make our world safe and prosperous again. I implore those of faith to renounce that faith if it requires you to hate and kill. My dearest wish for you all is freedom, peace, and happiness."

Eric applauded with his compatriots.


**************

At mid-afternoon, King Gnogoly and his Knights departed for the Isle of L'Áscarle. The Serasyan Knights and volunteers set off for Asyann—Larkin remained.

In the Great Hall, Eric gathered with the King's inner circle. Raulin sat on the edge of the dais. Alongside him King Guidion di Larkyn of Serasya, and the seven wizards of The Order of St Alúthien. Before him, at Eric's side stood Ryall and Aalys. On Eric's other side the remaining Elite guard, Clarice, and Haman. Sir Kilburn, Sir Albiron, and Sir Dowden stood to attention—hurt at the treachery of Sir Cesper etched on their faces. He had disobeyed Raulin's orders and sent the Oldegoth Fleets to patrol the Strait of Glimuth, a narrow waterway between Dorcliff and L'Áscarle. They had trusted him, even when he asked them to leave Castle Greycliff, not one had doubted his loyalty. They agreed he should remain while they gathered forces to defend the King. None had suspected he would open the drawbridge to Eald D'Árian's deadliest enemy. Sir Cesper languished in the dungeon, his fate undecided.

"My friends, the past weeks have tried you all and none lacked courage, ingenuity, and stamina. Those we loved and trusted inflicted upon us, our greatest wounds. I know it has been said that I am a weak King." Raulin rose and moved to stand before the throne, tension evident in the lines of his body. His long fingers traced the brass, carved wood and leather. "My father was a strong king. Feared. Hated by many, yes—but strong." He circled the throne, sighed and shook his head. "While he watched the populace with a gimlet eye, his closest friend cuckolded him. That friend impregnated his queen, and poisoned him—the one person my father chose to trust, murdered him!" The throne shook under a blow from Raulin's fist and a sob escaped Nutley.

Larkin rose and strode to Raulin's side.

"I won't—" Raulin swallowed and closed his eyes. Larkin's bracing arm across his shoulders calmed him. "I won't utter that name—I wish for all my people to forget him but remember his evil deeds."

Raulin smiled. "I'm much luckier in my friends than my father. I call each person in this room my friend and hope you see me in the same light."

"Come, Raulin." Larkin drew Raulin back to the edge of the dais. "Let us sit and talk, yes?"

Raulin resumed his seat on the dais, his head pivoted to Milo. "How is my brother?"

Milo cleared his throat and shrugged. "He'll recover. We are slowly weaning him off the laudanum. At the moment, he is strapped to his bed and the servants are massaging his cramping muscles."

"Good. When he is well enough, I wish to talk with him."

"Sire? What—"

"He is not my father's son, Milo, but he is my brother. If it is his wish, I will give him another chance."

"Your Majesty, do you honestly think he deserves yet another chance?"

"What would you have me do? Behead him? Throw him in the dungeons? How can I ask my people to be peaceful and kind if I am not prepared to be the same?"

Silence greeted his question.

"I am twenty-six years old, as is Larkin. We're both reluctant Kings, but we're Kings nonetheless. Our fathers both ruled by the sword and where did it get them?” Raulin bowed his head and sighed.

Larkin continued, “Work with us, help us change our world—make it safe for our children.”

Sir Kilburn cleared his throat. “What of Sir Cesper?”

Eric saw Raulin’s face darken. He grimaced and stared at the floor.

“He did far more damage than Randolf, but I will not put him to death. It is my guess he never chose to become a Wrigon-norce. I doubt he went willingly when Tagrali took him from the orphanage; I doubt any of them did. That he embraced his condition with such zeal is hardly surprising. A child who has nobody and suddenly made to feel valued would be easily coerced” The King shook his head; his shoulders sagged. “He can live out his days in a dungeon of Nutley’s choosing.”

Eric smiled sadly; those around him exchanged confused glances. Nutley alone knew which of the dungeons had escape hatches and more importantly, which did not.

The opening of a door broke the silence, a group of servants wheeled carts of food and wine in the door. Raulin and Larkin rose and began to serve the food.

“Wait!” Raulin spoke to the servants as they turned to go. “Please, stay and eat with us.”

The bemused servants shuffled back and received the first plates.

# 52

One year later. Eric clung to Tenebrozi as he swooped across the glassy millpond of King's Port Harbour, up to the battlements and over Castle Greycliff. The sun shone over the city. People's Day at the Dragon Coliseum filled the streets with hundreds of residents, eager to witness a tournament between Oldegoth, Serasya, and L'Áscarle. Eric would celebrate his first day off in months by riding in the Coliseum. Tenebrozi sailed low over the cheering people waiting for the doors to open—banked and landed outside the Ace's entrance.

Tenebrozi had chosen to stay with Eric, as his dragon. Azuria and Isuthiel lived at Tregaryon Hall with the Raigon-talth and served their kind on Dorcliff Island. Azuria the Healer monitored the wellbeing of dragons, both wild and domestic, all across Eald D'Árian. Isuthiel Green-fire rejected all titles as he governed the Dorcliff Channel and surrounding Islands. The wyverns had settled on the Rock of Allor, leaderless since the Rock of Wycliff fell, they still squabbled over control.

Eric shared his time between training new recruits for the King's Elite Guard and working with the Raigon-talth as they gently rehabilitated the surviving Wrygon-norce; when each regained their individuality they either returned home or stayed with the Raigon-talth to serve the world of Eald D'Árian. The wyvern blood in his veins had had no impact on Eric's character. The evil of those who served Tagrali wasn't inherent, rather cultivated by relentless indoctrination from childhood. Eric thanked his sister each day for removing him from Tagrali's reach. The rogue wizard did eventually find him but at a time when Eric had the wherewithal to fight back.

"Eric!" Larkin greeted him from among his guards; he held Telzoth's reins.

The green dragon turned his Emerald eyes to Eric. *'It is good to see you, Eric Man-dragon.'*

*'Greetings, Telzoth the Magnificent.'* "Larkin! It's great to see you, where is my sister?"

"She sends her love but with our baby only weeks away she didn't feel up to travelling."

"Is she well?"

Larkin face lit. "Glowing! She is very happy in her new home in Serasya."

"I'm glad to hear it. I'll come and visit very soon."

"We can wet the baby's head, no?"

"We will. How is everything in Serasya?"

"Prospering."

"And your brother, Prince Elyot, is he well?"

Larkin laughed. "Yes, he is to be married in the coming weeks. Kirya, the lovely young Wrigon-norce that Ryall returned to Asyann caught his eye. They are very much in love. But let us go and find Raulin before the tournament begins, yes? I believe he is inside the Coliseum."

Eric followed Larkin up the stairs to the King's private stall. Raulin entertained King Gnogoly and his consort, Gnigilly, the seven wizards, Ryall, Aalys, Prince

Randolf and a number of Oldegoth aristocrats. As Eric watched Randolf converse with a woman, he thought he looked weary though some colour had returned to his face.

Ryall rose and shook his hand. "Eric, are you ready for another stint on Dorcliff?"

"Yes, I look forward to it."

Ryall tilted his head toward Aalys. "By the way His Majesty is going, we may not have Aalys with us for much longer."

Eric discreetly watched as Raulin chatted to Aalys. "Romance blossoms?"

"It does. They only have eyes for each other—the rest of us will just have to talk among ourselves."

The commentator's voice resonated in the now full arena.

"Let's go, Eric." Larkin headed for the stairs. "We have a crowd to entertain."

Downstairs, Eric smiled and listened as Balien and Lucretia gave last minute instructions to their apprentice dragon ace, Yrian. Up the wide stairway the aces led their mounts and onto the launch platform where they climbed astride. Eric trailed Larkin on Telzoth the Magnificent into the arena. The crowd roared and Tenebrozi the Swift swooped low; two boys in the front row ducked and laughed as his wings whooshed over them.

THE END

# Glossary

**OLD ENGLISH**

Agraw – horrified

Afterling An inferior

Aweg – away

Bellytimber – food

Beek – bask

Bespawl – to spit or dribble

Blashy – weak beer

Bod (boddles) – bid

Blutter – blurtout

Brangle – squabble

Blore – bellowed

Blutter – speak rubbish

Breedbate – create strife

Carked – fretfully anxious

Clotterpot – stew

Conk – die.

Crug – food

Dalcop – dull headed

Dagian - dawn

Drassocked – untidy

Dringle – linger, waste time

Fadoodle – nonsense

Faffle – gust

Firefanged – burnt, overcooked

Flosh – swamp.

Frush – crush strike break.

Fnast – pant, snort.

Flachet – a sword

Fus – prepare.

Gallybagger – Ugly, strange and grotesque

Gang-toothed – protruding teeth

Gilly-wet-foot – swindler

Givel – heap up

Glop – eat (greedily)

Gofe – pillory

Graff – dig

Gundygut – glutton

Ha-ha trench – a steep-sided trench dug around a settlement for enemies to fall into (Often used as a latrine)

His Nibs – archaic word for a king (His Majesty)

Hufty-tufty – braggert

Hoddypeak – simpleton, blockhead

Hum – strong liquor

Hoful – careful

Jubbe – A large vessel for liquor

Kee-kaw – upside down

Lickspigot – fawning, servile

Lip snogged the hare's foot – late for dinner

Mawwallop – a badly cooked mess of food

Metrop – city

Muckender – napkin

Nyle – fog or mist

Ongle – claw

Pickaroon – mischief-maker

Pinion-razed – wing broken

Quetch – writhe in agony.

Reelpot – one who makes the drinks go around (waiter)

Roak – mist.

Rooped – hoarse, to have a cold

Ructus – belch

Sceaft – a smooth, round stick

Scrow – sky

Shreds – clothes.

Sloomy – lazy or dull

Snogged the hare's foot – late for dinner

Snotter-clout – handkerchief

Straight fingered – thoroughly honest, up standing.

Squint-a-pipes – squinty eyed

Tuzzy-muzzy – bouquet

Wandought – impotent

White livered – coward

Whoopub – hubbub

Whiddershins – unlucky

Wink-a-peeps – eyes

Yarken – prepa

# BIOGRAPHY

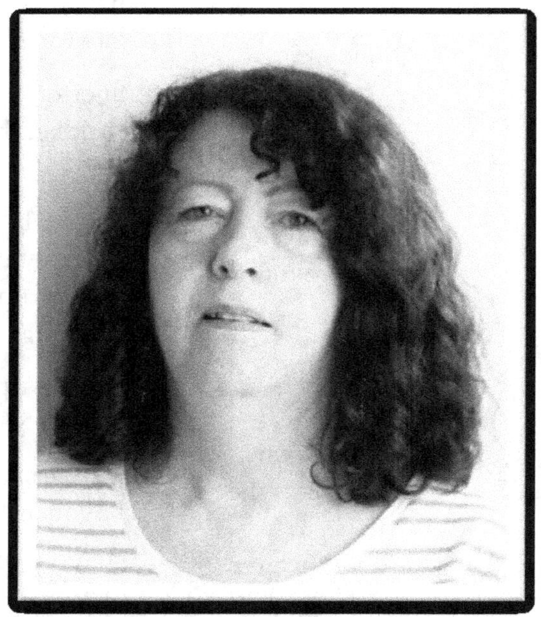

A. Isobel Sutcliffe lives in Western Queensland, Australia with her husband, two dogs and two cats. She has an adult son and daughter. A child of grazier parents, she grew up in remote rural Queensland. She spent thirty-three years working as a musician, playing in pubs and nightclubs. A visual artist she turned to writing in 2015.

For more of Ms Sutcliffe's work, go to
www.jacolpublishing.com